HIDING OUT

decoys by jonathan messinger

illustrations by rob funderburk

featherproof
BOOKS

There's such freshness, naturalness, humor and charm to Jonathan Messinger's stories—an overall sense of immediacy that planted me in the present—that only in retrospect did I realize how in *Hiding Out*, Messinger had also subtly constructed a personal and original world. –**Stuart Dybek**, author of *The Coast of Chicago* and *I Sailed With Magellan*

One part *Office Space*, one part George Saunders, one part Steve Martin's *Lonely Guy*, and one part Richard Yates' *Eleven Kinds of Loneliness*: shake it up, and what you have is a wholly original concoction. Hilarious at times, heartbreaking at others, Jonathan Messinger's *Hiding Out* is always, always surprising. These are fantastic stories by a writer whose next book I'm already eager to read. –**John McNally**, author of *The Book of Ralph* and *America's Report Card*

Hiding Out touches softly (and often painfully) on the intimacies and embarrassments of usually ordinary lives, revealing the way these lives open briefly into extraordinary gestures. Add to that slight cracks in the surface of reality and you have a phalanx of stories that weave their way through reality by simultaneously staring in at the hidden tender heart of things and gazing out at the fantastic always lurking beyond the real. An impressive debut. –**Brian Evenson**, author of *The Open Curtain* and *The Wavering Knife*

This is a vastly creative and compassionate book; filled with stories that explore the ways our dreams, our secret fantasies and fears, often intrude on our real lives to hilarious and heart-breaking effect. In story after story, Messinger peeks behind the curtain of the everyday to reveal the wondrous and terrifying possibilities of the human imagination. He is that rarest of finds: a writer whose feats of invention simultaneously dazzle and inspire. Go on. Turn the page and take a peek. You won't be sorry. –**Scott Snyder**, author of *Voodoo Heart*

Stories in this book have appeared in *Other Voices*, *Chicago Reader*, *Punk Planet*, *Resonance*, *THE2NDHAND*, *The Shore*, *Rainbow Curve*, *The Printers' Ball*, *Same Title Different Story* and read live at The Dollar Store.

This Story of 50 Words Feels as Though It Ran a Little Long, Maybe by 5 Words

There is little left for Connie to do. Her options: exhausted. Her headlights: dimmed. Her friends: silent. She lets slip her car keys onto the floorboard and neutralizes the gears. The dark car lacks any resistance, overwhelming her with its speed as it rolls downhill. She thinks of no lovers.

Published by
featherproof books
Chicago, Illinois
www.featherproof.com

First edition
∞

Library of Congress Control Number 2007924120
ISBN: 0-9771992-3-1
ISBN 13: 978-0-9771992-3-5

Cover photo: Nathan Keay, www.nathankeay.com
Illustrations based on Nathan's "Fitting In" series

Set in Baskerville

Printed on demand

For my friend Mark,
who is missed

TABLE OF CONTENTS

CAPTAIN TOMORROW

That summer our basement smelled of eucalyptus and pot roast. My mother was in massage therapy school and my sister Johanna and I would spend our afternoons watching weird old movies my grandmother left behind—or ones Johanna scored at flea markets and thrift stores—and eating leftovers from the night before. Most of the movies we watched were black-and-white love stories, or comedies with jokes that had died long before we were born. The VCR was new then. Pausing was a real novelty.

I was 13 and couldn't drive yet, so on a cool day in June I walked home from the corner store where I'd stolen us a few candy bars and two *TV Guides*. The mist in the air made me feel like I was sweating, though I walked slowly around the empty park and up the slow slope to our house.

When I got home, Johanna was still out. On the kitchen table was a note from our mother. She had school all day. She'd call when she could. She'd be home for dinner. We should get our rooms ready. She loved us.

I went downstairs and flipped on a video game. I was obsessed with an adventure game called Captain Tomorrow. I was a little guy in a bright white astronaut suit, blasting my way past aliens on the moon and eating green cheese for power-ups. There were supposedly ten levels, but I could only get past five. At the end of each level were moon dragons. Back then, every game had you fighting dragons.

I got to the end of level five and had some decisions to make. I could either eat a bunch of moon cheese and power up for the big battle, or I could not eat, which, in video game astrophysics, would make me lighter so I could jump higher around the level six Moon Dragon. The trick was to find the perfect balance.

"Holy shit, Alex!" Johanna yelled as she came running into the house. "I just went to this crazy zine convention in Jamaica Plain."

"Sounds stupid," I said. But she ignored it and raced down the stairs to hug me. Johanna was 16 and starting to show signs of hippieness; a strip of her blond oak hair had begun to dread up, and she'd quickly slid it through a psychedelic bead. She told me about the zine and video set she'd bought at the convention because she thought a goth kid and his little velvety handsewn goth zine were cute. She'd forgotten the zine in the car. After some discussion of whether we should watch the tape now or wait for me to finish— "You know you'll die," she said—I shut off my game.

I clunked the tape into the VCR and she put a finger in my face: "This is going to blow your mind," she said. "You might be too young for this, dude."

The screen flickered on and, without any titles or credits or opening music, we began watching people jump off of buildings; an entire tape of people leaping, without parachutes, from great heights.

"What the fuck did you buy?" I asked, but she didn't answer. Neither of us could stop watching. Just jump after jump. People plummeting. But after a while, it became clear that no matter how hard they tried to hide it, the jumps were stunts. There were a lot of awkward edits where guys—and they were always guys—would step off ledges. Then their bodies were on the ground, fake blood spoiling in the sun.

Johanna was into it. She took out a one-hitter and ground some weed into the tip. The smoke pushed the smells of our basement into old man–dungeon territory. On-screen, a guy jumped from atop a ten-story building, and the body on the ground looked just like it did when he was alive.

"Come on," I said. "There's no way this is real. That guy's brains should be on the sidewalk."

She passed me the bat and I smoked it like it was no big deal. We went on watching sad comedians throw themselves off buildings for laughs, and it made me wonder why, in the black-and-white days of entertainment, everyone thought it was funny to either fall or almost fall.

"Where did you get those candy bars and *TV Guides*?"

"I bought 'em at the store," I said.

She unwrapped a Three Musketeers while I fell asleep.

When I woke up, the video was on pause and Johanna was opening the one window we had in the basement, a tiny rectangle that came ajar like a miniature drawbridge. She had a fan pressed to the screen, trying to get rid of the pot smell.

"She's never going to come down here," I said. "She's going to have to eat and run."

"Well, let's get our shit together and do what we have to," she said. We held hands as we walked up the stairs, through the dining room, up the stairs to the second floor and into our respective rooms. Our mother was going to be home for dinner, before she went to work, and we were supposed to put all of our stuff in boxes so we could move the following week. I put four books and a shoebox of cassette tapes into a box before I got bored and went over to Johanna's room to watch her pack. Her room was twice the size of mine and everything in it seemed to be pegged to her personality. She'd painted the walls in green and blue stripes. Her pressed flowers hung from every corner. We should have seen the hippie thing coming.

"Mom's going to be pissed if you haven't done anything all day," she said, throwing old shoes into large empty boxes with resounding thuds. I lay down on her bed.

"I don't want to move," I said.

"That doesn't matter," she said. The truth was that I'd dreamed of moving. Our grandmother, who'd lived with us, had died the month before. She had been sick, but it still came suddenly. A hemorrhage. Johanna found her.

It was difficult not to find reasons to be sad in our house after that. There were memories attached to everything for our mom, who had grown up here. Once, she was making me a sandwich and when she opened a cabinet she just started sobbing, like she'd set off a tripwire.

"I want to move," Johanna said.

"Yeah, so do I."

"I know you do," she said. We acted like we knew everything about each other. When we were stoned, it was even worse.

Johanna held up a picture she'd taken from grandma's room. It was of grandma and her first husband, who was not our grandfather. About five years before our grandfather met her, our grandmother's husband went for a walk down some railroad tracks and threw himself in front of a train. Everyone declared it an accident, that he'd tripped and fallen before that, and that he just didn't get out of the way in time. But it seems unlikely. Everyone knows how to get out of the way of a train. Just step away.

"If this guy had been our grandpa, do you think we would look different?" Johanna pointed at him. He looked a little like a young Rodney Dangerfield.

"If that guy had been our grandpa, mom wouldn't be as pretty." We talked a lot about how pretty our mom was.

It was several rings before either of us realized the phone was ringing, and by then it was too late. We heard our mother's voice on the machine. She didn't have enough time between school and work. We should find some food to eat. There was plenty in the fridge. She loved us. She'd see us tonight.

We took it as a signal that we could beg off our duties.

"Let's go back downstairs and finish watching that movie," Johanna said, as though a string of suicides was some sort of story with an ending. In the basement, the smells of mom's massage oils and mediocre cooking enveloped us as we sprawled out on the old dark rug, sniffing the dust ground into it. We smoked some more weed. It took a long time to find the remote.

"Are you ready?" Johanna turned on the television, and the tubes warmed to the spot where we'd paused the tape. The screen was pitch black; we'd stopped it right between scenes, something neither of us realized at the time.

"Yeah, this is going to be awesome," I said, completely forgetting how bored I was before. Johanna pressed play and the black gave way to a black-and-white set of legs and shoes. They were high-heels, a woman's legs and dress tails.

"Holy shit," I said, and grabbed hold of Johanna's hand. I felt like I could cry.

The camera panned up and it was a typical woman of the 1940s, full and beautiful with artificially curly hair and subtle makeup. She looked like a woman from a home economics textbook of that era, in the modern life section, standing in the kitchen with her family. The camera pulled back and the image got a bit grainier, but it looked like she was about 15 stories up. Johanna fidgeted. Sweat glued our hands together. I could feel her bones.

The woman's knees bent slightly, into parentheses, and like it was nothing, like it was riding a bike, she jumped. And for the first time, the camera followed her. We watched as she fell, heavy against her dress flowing up behind her in waves. It looked like, even if Johanna pressed pause, nothing could stop it. It was inevitable. She hit the ground and that was it. She didn't move. And nothing we expected would happen did, just a little blood on the sidewalk. Neither of us said anything.

"Was that real?" I asked, but Johanna just let go of my hand and shut off the VCR.

"That fucking goth kid," she said. "I'm going to make a sandwich." I followed her up the stairs, but she turned to me:

"Why don't you just stay down here? Play video games or something."

"Was that real?" I asked again, but she was up in the kitchen not listening. "Well then make me a sandwich, too," I yelled, sitting back down. For a long time, I just stared at the black screen, thinking about that woman. How could someone's death be recorded like that? Did she ask for it? I thought about my mother, grieving over her dead mom. Does that sort of thing heal or hurt?

Just so I would stop thinking about it, I launched into a game of Captain Tomorrow. I roamed the moon looking for a princess who had been kidnapped, firing moonbeams at aliens who got in my way. I whipped through three levels before I realized how hungry I was.

"Where's my sandwich?" I yelled. Quiet. "Johanna!" Nothing.

Level four, with the dreaded moon caves: conquered.

On level five, I killed time so I didn't have to face the end. I ran around, scrolling the screen back and forth and tucking myself into a ball to roll along the craters. Just as I was about to reach the cliff where, if I jumped off, I'd have to land and fight the level five moon dragon, I spied a cloud in the corner of the screen. I jumped onto it and was awarded a free life. And then another one, and another one. And there was my guy, this little white blur, stuck in mid-air, on a cloud that shouldn't have been there in the moon's empty sky, racking up free lives. There was nothing I could do about it. It just got faster and faster. And pretty soon, I had so many lives, I could have played that game for the rest of my real life.

"What is that noise?" Johanna asked, coming down with a grilled cheese on a plate for me.

"I got a bunch of free lives," I said. "I'm invincible."

Johanna didn't laugh, just put down the plate beside me and lay down with her head on my shins. She pulled out her one-hitter and loaded it again. The phone rang, but we were mesmerized by our good fortune, all those extra chances. The answering machine picked up.

It was our mother. She was going out for a drink after work. She wouldn't be home until late. We should be in bed by midnight. She loved us.

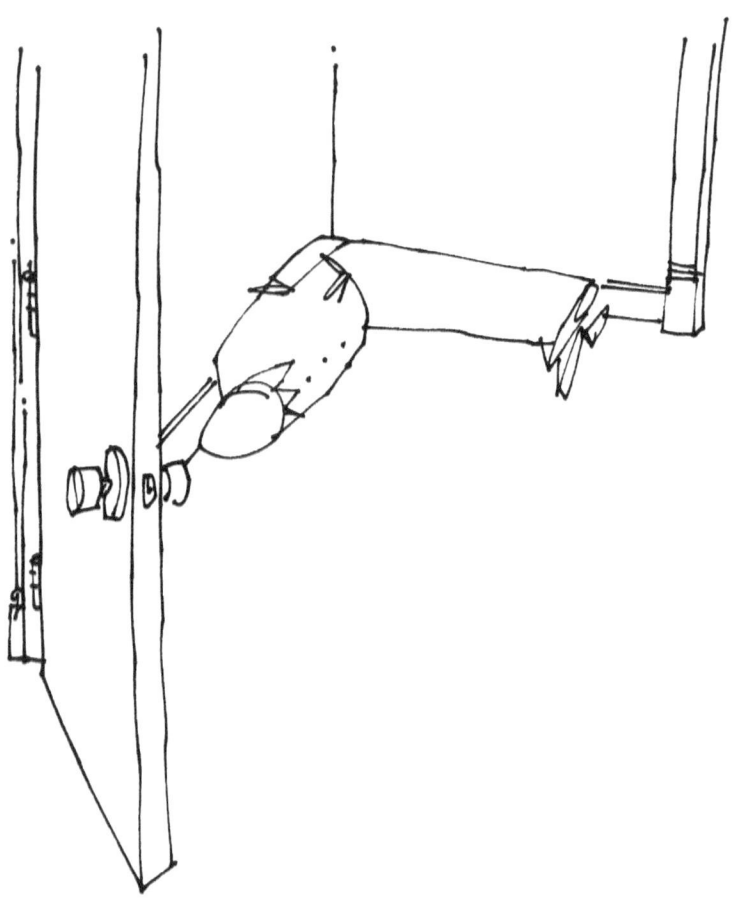

BICYCLE KICK

It's all because of my poor reflexes. A case of having little physical skill, sure, and maybe a short attention span. But there I was, hungover on a Sunday morning, in one of those indoor sports facilities that you never think you'll see the inside of, with the walled soccer fields and artificial turf like hot steel wool. Huge pictures of athletes you've never heard of adorn the walls, tricking you into thinking you look like them. But you don't, you look like me; tired and still not entirely clear on why you're playing in this league, some five games into the season. Unshaven, unenthusiastic, nearly undead. My headache, the one from the hangover, had me running in zig-zags. Every time I turned I would flinch and my body would lurch in another direction. So it wasn't a surprise, in retrospect. It took me off-guard, but I should have known it would happen.

There was a guy on the other team wearing the Brazil national team jersey—it didn't even say Ronaldo on the back—it was some obscure player I found out later, the guy was such a fan. But for a moment, I stared at the back of his jersey, at the name, Azofeifa. Such a name, Azofeifa. Beats the name on the back of my T-shirt, Terry. I was staring at the name Azofeifa, wondering if this guy, Azofeifa, if he could possibly be on the Brazilian team, his shorts blue and new enough, his socks pulled high enough. And as I was thinking this, just watching him, Azofeifa—such a name!—wondering if I was in the presence of greatness and playing against a World Cup competitor, as this thought crossed my mind I saw the ball emerge, in the air, in my peripheral vision, and I saw Azofeifa take two confident strides away from me and then, something magical happened—and I'd like for you to understand the magic of it before I tell you the consequences, because the magic is the best part—Azofeifa took two confident strides away from me, and as the ball knuckled through the air, no spin at all, just a flat and boring thing, I watched Azofeifa leap, his left leg kicking in front of him like a ballerina, and I noticed that his thigh muscle, I believe it's called a quadriceps, was of such girth and animal litheness that I quivered, but then, his torso realigned, so it looked like he was reclining in the air, parallel to the ground, just buffeted by the wind, gravity at the whim of Azofeifa, and as his left leg hastened back down he lifted his right so that it emerged above him, an obtuse angle on the Azofeifa plane, and again with the suppleness of the quad, and the kick, connecting with the ball and sending this object, appearing two-dimensional before he touched it but now, in Azofeifa's universe it was a living thing, spinning with a celestial speed and growing larger by the second, it could only be described as magic, this bicycle kick that defied physical laws in a most real way, and the ball now coming alive and growing so large that it was there, in front of my face, and here we see the consequences of my momentary obsession with Azofeifa, my reflexes so poor, my headache so monstrous, my fleeting love for Azofeifa so pure, that I couldn't even shutter my eyelids, and the ball hit my bare yellow eyeball and it is here, of course, that I stop remembering.

I tell you this because it explains just how important Azofeifa is to my current condition, both physical and mental. My team, acquaintances from work and their friends and some other people I would never associate with if I actually associated, rushed me to the hospital. I came to in the emergency room, waking up stuck to a vinyl chair, surrounded by coughing and bleeding people sensibly dressed in winter parkas and boots. I in my indoor track shoes, Umbro shorts and ratty T-shirt with my name on the back. It was quite a shock, and I yelped a bit, which I think got me in to see the doctor quicker than even the guy both shivering and sweating, who looked like his skin was possibly falling off. I looked so bad on account of the hangover and the bare eyeball contact that this man nodded at me to go past. The doctor, a quack, I'm sure, calling himself Dr. Owen and not telling me if that was his first or last name so I couldn't know if he was being cute or not, said I was probably fine, which I knew. But, he said, it would be important to take a CAT scan, an expensive procedure that my insurance would largely cover and would ensure that there wasn't any hemorrhaging anywhere, that my retina was intact, and that various other side effects of being smashed in the bare eyeball were not in effect. I agreed.

I fell asleep in the CAT scan, which I don't think you're supposed to do, especially if you might have a concussion, as I might have had, but Dr. Owen didn't notice. When it was through, I sat in a station just off the nurse's desk, where I could watch them mark and erase names on a giant whiteboard. Every erasure brought with it an anxiety. I had to listen hard to ensure it wasn't because someone had died, that the patients here were just being dispatched, but not to the grave. Someone down the hall in Bed 8 was labeled Knife Shoulder. I saw my name under Bed 3—Soccer Head, it read. I liked that. I noticed that in Bed 11, listed on the chart just below mine, it read Baby Trauma, and I decided to stop reading. My right eye was bandaged, and I made a game of pressing down around the socket, to determine where it hurt most. I wondered where my teammates were. A few of them had been beside me when I'd awakened and yelped, but they didn't follow me into the scan. I decided not to ask the nurses to fetch them.

Dr. Owen arrived after a long time, long enough to make me think I'd been forgotten, Soccer Head in Bed 3 now so permanent on the whiteboard they'd have to use vinegar to wipe me out. The doctor was tall in a 19th-century way, slightly stooped and with glasses just slightly larger than his eyes. A white idea of a beard played along his chin, wispy and ugly.

"I have good news and I have bad news," he told me. "And the bad news is more complicated, so I'm going to give you the good news first."

This seemed to me a fair deal.

"The good news is that you don't have a concussion, and other than a weird-looking shiner, on account of your eye being open on impact, no major damage at all."

This was good news. I was happy my head had made it out OK. Dr. Owen started in on the bad news. The CAT Scan had shown I had an unusual condition in my head. Two aneurysms, side-by-side. Two bloated blood vessels that could, given enough emotional or physical stress, burst, sending squid clouds of blood over my brain, erasing thoughts, functions, memories—irreparable damage. Highly unusual, to have two such advanced aneurysms so close together, he assured me, as if I should be proud. Like I was up for the Guinness Book.

"Normally, if we had caught one aneurysm, I'd say we should open up your head and get it out," he said. "It's not an easy procedure, but it's safer than walking around with a time bomb up there. But if we did that in your case, we'd be in danger of rupturing the second aneurysm, and the whole procedure would be for naught."

I closed my left eye, but kept my right one, behind the bandage, open. I liked the fuzzy darkness. It built an incomprehensible wall around my head that kept me from concentrating.

"Do you want to see the scan?" Doctor Own asked.

"No, I don't wanna—why would I wanna—I don't," I said.

"OK," he said. "But in case you're curious, it looks like two snakes swallowed rabbits then crawled inside your head."

I heard him pick up the scan, but I kept my left eye shut so I wouldn't have to see it.

"Suit yourself," Dr. Owen said, obviously disappointed.

I wasn't quite clear on what he was telling me, and it annoyed me that I had to ask.

"So am I the walking dead, then?" I asked. "How many months?"

"Well, no one can really tell you that. These things, people die of natural causes with them still intact, still in their heads. Others rupture at any moment; anything can do it, really. You could live the rest of your natural life as well as anyone else, or you could take two steps away from me and fall to your death."

It was no help, precisely zero information. The news had emptied me and Dr. Owen gave me nothing to fill that space. He just stared off down the corridor, like he was marking the moment I'd drop.

"Will I have any side effects, any dizziness or blindness or headaches?"

"Nothing's for sure. You'll likely get headaches, but do you get headaches now?"

I said I did.

"Then you won't notice a difference."

"What about loss of memory, paralysis—should I stop drinking?"

He told me that I didn't have to worry about those, that I should cut back on the drinking, and that he would prescribe a blood thinner for me.

"So there are no ill effects?" I asked.

"Well, as I said, you could die."

I looked him in the eye, my one good eye flicking back and forth between the two of his.

"So, if you had to give me odds for living another forty years, say until I was 70, what would the odds be?"

"I'm not very good at that sort of thing."

"10 to 1? 100 to 1?"

"I've never really understood what that means," he said.

"Just give me the odds."

"Of you living till you're 70?" he said. "I'd say it's 35-75."

I shook my head. Dr. Owen and his 19th-century frame, blunt disregard for my need to be reassured and fucked-up math was too much. This man was making my world small. I imagined he was a moon who had just eclipsed me.

I walked into the waiting room and saw that the team had left. I walked out onto the sidewalk and stared at the sun, out of my one good eye. I imagined Azofeifa, so fleet and at ease in his body. My feet felt magnetized, drawn to the core of the earth, leaden. I tried to imagine that gravity was pulling my blood down, sucking it back out of the swollen ice-purple bruise around my right eye, out of the one aneurysm, and then out of the other. Things moved inside me, as I stood still, my feet pulling down.

At the bar, later that afternoon, with the team all still wearing their T-shirts and all buying me beer after beer and slapping me in the shoulder once they got drunk enough to stop treating me like porcelain, with everyone there with their names across their backs exalting at having gotten out of the game before they lost, thanks to my eye injury, I couldn't decide if I should tell them. It's not really a topic for bar conversation, or that's exactly what it is, but not this type of bar conversation. I wanted to sit down with somebody, didn't matter who, sit down across from each other at a table not too far from the jukebox, and sip a beer and tell them that this could be the last beer of my life, or it could be just another, I would never know. And the whole thing made me feel stupid, like I was writing a poem for a high school literary magazine. I'd think it was important and deep but the grammar would be all wrong and adults would secretly laugh at me. I wanted to change the name on the back of my T-shirt, or I wanted to keep it exactly the same but be somewhere where no one knew it, or I wanted the people who surrounded me in the bar to remember it without having to secretly lean back and read it, or I wanted to be Azofeifa, spin off into the Azofeifa orbit, free in a different way. I stood up from my bar stool and planted my feet on the floor, the magnets returning, draining that blood out of my brain, the aneurysms thinning, the rabbits emerging whole from the snakes' mouths and bicycle kicking, their little rabbit feet flipping through the air. I closed my good eye and opened my bad one and stared out into the fuzzy darkness around me, the atmospheric wall built by me, built out of my slow reflexes, my brief and weird obsessions, my inability to react, and I wondered what I would do next.

I sat at home all week. I ate what I wanted, watched what I drank and took Dr. Owen's blood thinners often, but with no regularity. I enjoyed them. I'd take four at a time and watch as the wall on the other side of the room blurred, though I didn't know if that was a result of the blood thinners or not, so I conducted control experiments, gazing at the wall when off my meds. It never blurred. The effect was different, too. Sober, I found myself staring at the wall like it was a traitorous ex-lover, the light tufts of my eyebrows canopying my vision. On the blood thinners, it just blurred, and I would stare at it for hours, relaxing, and ignore the ringing phone and the shaking voice of my boss on the answering machine. I'd quit, he just didn't know it yet. I'd quit by not showing up. By the end of the week it was the same to him, but my accident must have kept me in some good graces at the office, which made me smile when I thought of it, my teammates now out of their uniforms and in their suits, rallying behind me, asking the boss to give me one more chance, describing my black eye and the way I'd yelped in the emergency room and how I'd tried my best to play it cool at the bar, and that my injury must have been my excuse. I liked that.

They were all happy to see me when I showed up for the next Sunday's game. I hadn't come to play, of course, and I felt like an imposter standing among the cleated athletes in mesh shorts and me in my corduroys and sweater. Or I felt like the world had been righted, that I'd finally been outed as not one of them, as an other, a sheep in wolf's clothing. Of course, I was there to see Azofeifa, to confront the one intangible in my life that felt confrontable. They thought I'd come to play, and one of them even said to me, "Terry, man, you're the toughest little guy I've ever known and I'm proud you're on our team." I wondered if he'd rehearsed it, or if he was making fun of me. But I smiled.

Then he said, "So are you OK to play? Because we thought maybe you weren't going to so we asked a friend of ours. I hope that's OK."

"It's cool," I said. "I'm here to see someone else."

He looked at me strangely, nervous like I'd discovered a secret. I looked over his shoulder and saw why. I hadn't noticed the new guy until now, as if he were summoned by my teammate's words, an apparition hovering with the rest of the team, juggling the ball on his head, knees and feet, striking in even intervals like a metronome, hypnotic almost, in its failure to reveal any imperfection. He looked just like me. I know I may be the only one to actually say it, to have the insight to recognize it, but he looked just like me had I gone down a different path, his clothes hanging from his body like a mannequin's, his hair lustrous but in place, his muscles in complete control and his body trim from proper diet. It was like looking into an alternate universe and discovering it preferable to the one you occupy and then finding the portal sealed. Regret. It was all regret that consumed me, then. I'd remembered a story from an evening news show about identical twins; in one of the segments they showed two twin sisters, one a physical trainer and the other a smoker and drinker, and they could not have looked less alike. Cousins, maybe, but not twins. And the out-of-shape one, the one who clearly was going to die sooner, told the newsman that she had no regrets, that she'd chosen her life and she'd found pleasure in other things, while her sister found it in fitness and the like. I knew then that she was lying, because all I had were complaints and a long span of idling that began I don't know when and would continue until those aneurysms popped and my brain sunk into itself. I didn't know where this bogeyman came from, but it was too much. I retreated, and my teammate made no effort to stop me.

Forgetting myself, I bent at the water fountain to sip before I got in my car and left, determined to do something for the first time since I'd received the news. When I rose I saw him,

Azofeifa, walking down the hallway to the field, no doubt scouting other teams, or maybe warming up before his game, a full hour's regimen of stretching and lunging to prepare some of his magic tricks. I remembered why I was there. I stopped him. I had to.

"Hey," I said. He just looked at me.

"I'm the guy. The guy who you hit in the eye last week, with that spin kick."

"Oh yeah." His voice registered two octaves below mine. I felt it in my jaw.

"Check it out, my black eye."

"Uh huh."

"I went to the hospital. You'll never believe this. I have two aneurysms."

"I'm not paying your bills."

I hadn't expected this, obviously. I'd thought we'd have a good laugh. *Check out what your superhuman abilities have wrought.* I wasn't angry with him, certainly.

"That's not what I meant."

"It's not my fault."

"I know. The doctor said it could have been up there all my life, for all he knew." It was true, but I had the feeling I was just saying anything to keep him there. I wanted to get control.

"OK."

"So in some ways, I'm thankful to you, because now I know."

"OK."

We just stared at each other. I realized that the weight of what I was telling him wouldn't allow him to just walk away. I'd told him about my serious medical condition, and now social graces dictated that he talk with me until I excused him. I reveled in it.

"Yeah, so it's interesting. I don't know what to do about it. I mean, I can't have surgery, and I could live a long life with these guys up in my head, or I could die right now."

"Uh huh."

He was sweating, Azofeifa, I could see the gleam along his brow and even a disgusting, muddy condensation on his upper lip. He may have thought I still contemplated suing, but it may have just been the horror of what I was telling him. Sweat was appropriate. There was something beautiful about his sudden reduction, even if I was already becoming nostalgic for a time when he was perfect.

"So what do you think? What should I do?"

"I don't know."

I stared at him until he thought about it more, the sweat now coming down like we were on the soccer field.

"What's the big deal? Just live the way you always live and if you die tomorrow you die tomorrow. I could die tomorrow, too. I could walk right out of here and get hit by a bus."

"But that's a cliché," I said. "People don't get hit by buses that often."

"Yeah."

He was coming around, I could feel it.

"But for me," I said, "there's an invisible, silent bus always right behind me, and I don't know when it's going to run me over."

Azofeifa seemed to take this extension of his cliché seriously.

"My first thought would be I'd try to kill myself," he said. "Knowing all that would probably drive me crazy."

I thought about this, how for someone like Azofeifa, so keenly physical that the slow erosion of his body would be too much to handle, the imminence of death, both present and vague, would be too much for him.

"It would," I said.

Azofeifa and I looked away from each other. I could tell that it was over. Now that he'd revealed himself to me, that I'd seen his weakness as he'd previously exposed mine, we were no longer bound to each other. We could part as friends.

"You can't play soccer anymore, huh?"

"I don't think it'd be a good idea."

"Yeah."

He'd stopped sweating, and he looked exhausted and yellow beneath the old fluorescents of the indoor sports arena's hallway lighting. It was time for us to go.

"Good luck today," I said.

"You too, with everything."

He walked away slowly, a drained and limp version of the previous week's Azofeifa. I felt renewed, content to have so few strings to cut loose, so few physical desires. The regret was still there, but I thought that when it was over, those regrets wouldn't be what I'd have in front of me, not anymore. I walked out of the arena into the sunlight, the cold air and the dirty sparkle of car hoods. I popped four blood thinners and waited for the dizziness to come, just to see how it felt.

HIDING OUT

Eamon Peterson is lonely. He has tried to cure his loneliness, but has run out of ideas. It is a compound problem. He has failed even in the idea department.

Eamon plays Euchre on Yahoo! Games, he reads blogs written by people he does not know. He admires the women on tittytajmahal.com, wondering how there are so many women paid to have sex on camera, and yet he cannot meet a woman during his daily commute or his long excursions to the pizza shop. The supply of women performing any manner of sex act on his computer is inexhaustible. They are always new.

Eamon works as a file librarian for a hedge fund company. Contained in such a file is a stranger's investment history, marital status and history, military history and, it seems, the most personal information one could imagine. Hopedale calls its corporate espionage "business intelligence," robbing it of its cinematic cool. One potential client is Eamon's favorite: Gilbert Madden has consummated three extramarital affairs, instigated turbulence in an African diamond exporter and eats one pint of chocolate ice cream before falling asleep each evening. Reading this man's dossier amplifies Eamon's loneliness. Here is a man living an outrageous life, one too scandalous for his company. Conversely, Eamon feels he was hired precisely because he would never be so scandalous. He lacks the potential.

The library is covered in a low-pile gray carpet, the kind that feels like tree bark on the palms. The file cabinet drawers are longer than Eamon is tall, and they reach the ceilings, as though they are load bearing. The library has a counter, at which Eamon sits with his laptop, facing a hallway and receiving requests. Eamon often allows himself to wander back into the corner, where the last row of drawers faces the beige wall, and lay on his back for a brief nap. If anyone truly needs him, the ring of the bell on the counter or the electronic clamor of the keycard opening the library's door is more than enough to rouse him. He simply pushes hard the bottom drawer, as though he has just slotted another file, and rises to meet the interloper. No one catches him. He quietly enjoys his job: It furnishes him with a good salary and little stress.

Mostly, though, he stares at his computer, sitting high on his ergonomic stool with his elbows on the counter. He reads every e-mail he receives, including the advertisements sent from the many mailing lists to which he subscribes, and those sent by the pre-approved sponsors of the many newspaper websites for which he has registered. He reads them all. He reads the ads for Anatrim, a miracle slimming drug that speaks of its quickness in a language once reserved for immortals. He reads the penis enlargement and the sex stamina e-mails more than once, chuckling to himself over the bizarre syntax of shady promises.

He reads one now. The subject is: "Oh, you do it very fast," and the body of the e-mail reads: "Good day to you bro! Go and tell her you're not among those who try to combat this for years. Now with Extra Time. Lack control over your squirting? You won't hear another word of reproach from her! She'll just keep you a secret from her friends!"

Eamon develops a new game. He writes himself e-mails—from his work account to his personal—every half hour. He checks his personal e-mail just twice during the workday and is surprised by the number of messages he has dispatched. Often, it seems more than possible. The content is predictable. Most are exhortations to better himself: Get out of the house more. Meet more people. Be less awkward. Occasionally he writes his own SPAM, targeted at himself:

```
Date: Wed, 6 Sep 2006 11:23:55 (-0700)
From: Epeterson@hdcapital.com
To: aymon@hotmail.com
Subject: fantasy baseball is fake!

Hello young'un! Stop checking your team's stats! Get
into plank position and flatten those abs! Trouble
```

```
with jelly belly no more. You'll cut steaks on your
stomach no time flat. Flat!
```

Eamon has become his own pen pal. He thinks of this as he opens the refrigerator of the office kitchen and is confronted, once again, with the reality that someone has taken his lunch. This had been a problem for Eamon in the past, but he thought his recent strategy of bringing what he termed "defensive lunches" had solved the problem. Rather than cold pizza or canned soup, Eamon substituted unidentifiable meats and soups contained in plastic bags. Today, he'd brought a bag of ham. A simple, clear sack of pink meat, dewy on the inside from when he'd bagged it hot. It is gone. The only employee in the employee kitchen is Rachael Morneau, a woman of his own young age. She is wearing a light, flowery dress, something that strikes Eamon as a dress women don't wear to work, but rather on vacation. Eamon has searched for Rachael Morneau on Google Image, hoping to miraculously find naked pictures of her. Nothing appears but a few images of her crossing the finish line at charity 5Ks.

He says hello to her for the first time he can remember. He's never initiated anything with her. He's never shown initiative. She nods at him and smiles.

"This is weird, but did you see anyone take any ham?" Eamon asks.

"No."

"Shoot. Because I had a bag of ham in here and now it's gone."

"People here are such assholes."

"Thank you."

Eamon is stunned by his good fortune at finding a partner in commiseration with Rachael Morneau. He takes the elevator to street level and treats himself to a slice of deep dish pizza, sausage-stuffed. When he returns to the library, he opens his work e-mail and types the following:

```
Date: Thu, 7 Sep 2006 13:03:12 (-0700)
From: Epeterson@hdcapital.com
To: aymon@hotmail.com
Subject: stop pussying

Rachael Morneau sounds French! You can do it. What's
the worst that can happen, you say stupid things?
The stupidest thing is the thing unsaid. Say it.
```

He closes his laptop and retreats to the back of the library. On his back, he stares at the inoffensive fluorescent lamp hanging from the ceiling. His belly happily upset with sausage and cheese and the fiery acid of tomato sauce, Eamon closes his eyes with no expectation that he will actually sleep. He sighs a slight sigh; just narrow enough to accommodate the hem of a woman's dress.

Eamon Peterson is not obese, but the extra weight he carries often forces people to describe him as "ruffled." He cares about this deeply, though it was more of an undefined nag until Eamon decided he would woo Rachael Morneau out of her summer dress and into his heart. His e-mails to himself now betray an obsession. Rarely do they touch on any subject other than Rachael, or Eamon's appearance. Occasionally, they will concern other matters, such as lists of new bands Eamon feels he should know. But even these are now heavy with the weight of expectation, as though his future with Rachael were a trailer hitched to Eamon's thoughts. He reads another now:

```
Date: Tue, 12 Sep 2006 09:23:04 (-0700)
From: Epeterson@hdcapital.com
To: aymon@hotmail.com
Subject: not healthy

worried about your mindstate? Unsure of the line
between appropriate and inappropriate focus on the
female species? Be cool, bro. Be cool.
```

Eamon takes his lunch out of his backpack—a salad, an apple and an orange—and sits in the kitchen to eat it, alone. No one enters.

He returns to the library to find his phone ringing. He answers it.

"Dude, where you been?"

It's Eamon's boss, Dave, a red-haired man on the brink of 40. Dave always calls Eamon "dude" when no one is around. At first Eamon thought he did it to create a false sense of camaraderie, to make Eamon feel more comfortable. But he soon realized that Dave did it to fight the advance of aging. At company parties, Dave often cornered Eamon, called him "dude," discussed women and made him down shots, as though he had plugged Eamon into a role in a static script that a college friend once played—a type of jock Alzheimer's.

"Lunch," said Eamon.

"Birthday's coming up," said Dave. "Gotta make the jump."

Every year Dave throws himself a barbecue, invites a few friends, some of his staff and various family members. It's always the same for Eamon: great food, poor company. After an afternoon of running around the yard, putting back shots the way marathoners douse water cups, Dave jumps off the sloped roof of his house and onto the soft carpet of his backyard grass. Until he breaks a bone, he reasons, he's still a young man.

"You coming out?" asks Dave.

"Sure," says Eamon. "It's getting serious."

Last year, Dave sprained his left wrist. It swelled like paint on a rusting car.

"Don't worry. It's going to be tight."

Eamon says "OK" and hangs up the phone. Three seconds later it rings again.

"Dude! I wasn't finished!"

Dave tells Eamon that he has a stack of files he's sending with an intern.

"OK."

"That's all, I guess."

"Thanks."

"Dude, the jump's going to be awesome."

"I know."

Fifteen minutes pass, and neither files nor intern arrive. Eamon checks his e-mail.

```
Date: Tue, 12 Sep 2006 14:21:51 (-0700)
From: Epeterson@hdcapital.com
To: aymon@hotmail.com
Subject: Give it a shot

If you really want something to happen with Rachael,
you're going to have to make it happen. You can't
```

```
just let coincidences constantly bring you together.
It doesn't work that way. You need to be active.
```

Eamon does not remember writing this e-mail to himself. It seems unlike him to think so clearly. Confident that the files Dave spoke of will never arrive, he scuffles to the rear of the library and sits with his back to the wall. Before he falls asleep. Slumped in the corner, he thinks of that e-mail. He wonders when time began disappearing.

At lunch the next day, Eamon takes a walk. Walking calms him. He wonders if anyone else is calmed by the dodging of approaching bodies, the modular tension of passing slower pedestrians. Eamon walks for blocks, turning indiscriminately, knowing eventually he will stop to buy food. As he passes approaching women, he looks at their faces to see if he recognizes them. He assumes the women on tittytajmahal.com come from places like California or Florida, where women wear less clothing as a matter of course; the more naked, the closer to sex. Still, there's no reason to think any of these women in the Loop couldn't appear on his computer at some point, nude and in love with intercourse. Eamon walks the sidewalks looking at the women. He looks at one professional woman, gray houndstooth suit snooping out of a thin windbreaker. Her blond, highlighted hair is pulled back in a tight ponytail that makes the top of her skull look distended, like a landfill. Eamon thinks, *Sorry honey, but no thanks.* And then, *Where do I get off?*

Returning to the office he takes his stir-fry into the kitchen, and there is Rachael Morneau, sitting alone at a table, watching the MSNBC stock ticker scroll by, and a man whose face appears impossibly bloated discusses figures. Eamon sits at a different table.

"You can sit here," Rachael says. "I'm not really watching this."

"OK."

Eamon wonders if his food is too smelly. He hopes it doesn't intrude.

"So, whatever happened?"

"What?"

"To the case of the missing ham."

"Oh. Well, you solved it."

"I did?"

"You said: People here are such assholes."

"My first closed case."

Rachael and Eamon eat in silence. Rachael has a salad in front of her, which she dismantles leaf by leaf, her fork lowering and rising like a machine. She smiles when she catches Eamon looking at her.

"Is that enough food?" Eamon asks.

"Not really, but I have a race coming up."

"You can have some of my chicken if you want."

"Thanks."

Rachael's fork scoops two pieces of chicken and deposits them in her salad with the same robotic precision. She covers them with greens, as though she doesn't want to see herself eat them. When she chews, she smiles in a way that makes it appear she's surprised to find chicken in her salad.

"It's the least I could do," says Eamon.

"For what?"

"For solving the case of the missing ham."

"Brilliant," she says. "I'll take my payments in chicken."

Back at his desk, high on adrenaline and satisfaction, Eamon pays no attention to the three small towers of files pyramiding next to his computer. The conversation with Rachael was aphrodisiac. He misses her already.

He writes the following e-mail to himself:

```
Date: Wed, 13 Sep 2006 14:04:21 (-0700)
From: Epeterson@hdcapital.com
To: aymon@hotmail.com
Subject: perfecto

smooth operator. don't let anyone tell you different.
in just six short lunches, you could have her
charmed. boy, keep it up.
```

He presses send, closes his e-mail, eyes the architecture of work to his right, and is relieved when the phone rings.

"Mr. Peterson?"

Eamon does not recognize the voice on the other end.

"This is Gilbert Madden, president of Trance Outfitters."

"Hello."

"Ring a bell?"

The name rings a chorus of bells in Eamon's brain. This is the guy. This is the guy whose file Eamon has read one hundred times this week. He's the one who had sex with a mistress in the Pyrenees while on an illegal hunting trip. This guy's file is an adventure novel, the kind men with mustaches in the '70s would idolize.

"Yes, sir."

"I suppose it's highly unusual for someone like me to call you, yes?"

"Yes, it is."

In fact, Eamon has never had any contact with any of Hopedale's clients. His job requires only intra-office communication. He receives, files and distributes, nothing more.

"Well, you guys over there at Hopedale, you said you didn't want me investing with you. That's fine, I don't hold it against you, certainly not you in particular. You're the librarian, right?"

"Yes."

Gilbert Madden wants his file back. It doesn't matter to Eamon, Gilbert Madden says, how he knew to call Eamon, but it appears that Gilbert Madden doesn't want any loose ends.

"Are you in trouble?" asks Eamon.

"Not if I can help it," says Gilbert Madden.

"I don't know if I can help you."

"I intend to pay. Think about it."

And with that, the phone falls silent. No sound follows, and it is so quiet in the office, the receiver pressed to Eamon's ear makes a sound like the ocean. Or, he thinks, of a car perpetually passing him by.

Thursday. The phone rings.

"Dude. Saturday. Can you handle it?"

Dave's voice is reedy. It sounds like he's been screaming since yesterday morning.

"It's going to be intense, huh?"

"You know it."

"Who's going to be there?"

"The usual suspects. Dude. Starts at one. Jump's at six."

Eamon takes comfort from this, even if the usual suspects

are people he dislikes. At least they are known quantities. New files have been arranged to the right of his computer, again as a pyramid. Eamon takes the peak only, leaving a manila plateau behind. His shoes on the carpet sound like electronics, like he's a video game character. He sinks happily into a routine, finding empty green hanging folders to fill. Eamon wonders about these new people in his life: Rachael Morneau, the girl who, if all goes to plan, he will later claim he always knew was the girl of his dreams; Gilbert Madden, the tycoon of tenebrous ethical standing, a man of mystery who's worried his secrets will be revealed. Gilbert Madden, Eamon thinks, would know how to make Rachael Morneau his woman. And he would say it like that: "You're my woman." Eamon doesn't want to be Gilbert Madden, but he does want those powers. To use for good.

After completing his filing, he returns to his computer to check his e-mail. He reads the following:

```
Date: Thu, 14 Sep 2006 09:34:12 (-0700)
From: Epeterson@hdcapital.com
To: aymon@hotmail.com
Subject: Give it a shot

It's not like you see her all of the time. If it
didn't work out, you wouldn't have to save any face.
The worst that can happen is that you get embarrassed.
The best that can happen is that you fall in love.
Come on, loverboy. Do it! Take the plunge.
```

Eamon does not remember writing himself this e-mail. Again, its logic is so clear and propulsive, it seems impossible he could have written it. The effect is dizzying. What else, he wonders, what other actions is he taking during these blackouts? He reads through the other e-mails he's sent himself in the last few weeks, 16 a day. It's impossible to remember them all. He sends his friend Steve an e-mail, telling him his e-mail has been acting strange and he's wondering if Steve has received any odd messages from him. He refrains from e-mailing himself the rest of the day. At lunch, he eats in back. Pizza sauce gets on his shirt. His nerves are wrecked. He falls asleep.

Friday he calls in sick to see a doctor, but the doctor is busy. Eamon stays at home, visiting various websites who trade with tittytajmahal.com, like leonsmovies.com and assexprass.com. Eamon checks his work e-mail using the remote web service. Nothing from himself, just a message from Dave that proclaims Eamon had better not skip the next day's party. Its one line reads: "Dude, you better get all your puking out of the way now because tomorrow you're going to have to hold your liquor, fuckhead."

Eamon calls his work voice-mail and there's a message from Gilbert Madden. He doesn't say who he is, but Eamon recognizes the voice. Hearing it is like uncovering a repressed memory, or hearing someone else recount a story that happened to him. He wants to meet Eamon Monday night after work at The Exchequer, a dark bar in the South Loop with terrible food. Even high rollers have to keep low profiles, so they're both learning.

Eamon brings a 12-pack of Stella Artois to the barbecue. The day is surprisingly sunny and warm; everyone will be in shorts and long-sleeved jerseys. A 12-pack may be necessary on a day like this. When he arrives in Dave's backyard, Eamon sees all of the same people who were at the party last year. He's late. Everyone is here, and empty bottles have already begun to replace the full ones in their six-pack cardboard sleeves. Eamon looks around the backyard and has the feeling of stepping out of a home movie and entering it again five years later. Everyone looks older. The men's shirts stretch farther, the bags below the women's eyes shine with age-reduction cream. Neither technique is working. Dave, though, Dave is still running. He's wearing a Cubs hat and a T-shirt that features the character from the board game Operation and reads, I HAVE A BONE TO PICK WITH YOU.

"Dude! Finally!"

Dave wraps his arm around Eamon and takes the 12-pack in his hand at the same time.

"I'm not that late, am I?"

"It's 3 o'clock, dude! Dude! This guy," Dave says, now addressing the rest of the party, "played hooky yesterday. Called in sick. You don't look sick to me!"

Dave good-naturedly punches Eamon in the shoulder, but Eamon doesn't pay it any attention. Had he really slept so late that he's missed almost half of the party?

"Don't worry, though, I won't tell the boss!" Dave erupts into laughter as he thrusts one thumb below his sternum, to indicate to everyone he is the boss, in every sense. Everyone knows this already. No one laughs.

After some brief idle chat with people whose names Eamon always forgets, he parks himself against the back door to Dave's garage. He watches kids, cousins of Dave, play basketball on a small hoop. One of them, a small redhead that could be Dave's own kid, scores. When he does, he yells, "Touchdown!" and laughs to make up for all the laughter that is not occurring at the party. Eamon is jealous of the kid being a kid.

Rachael Morneau enters the gate through which Eamon had entered two hours ago. She's wearing the same sundress she wore to work the day she solved the ham caper. She carries a small basket in her hands. Eamon wonders if she meant to look like she stepped out of a painting. After Dave makes her do a shot of Jagermeister, which she thanks him for with a sour smile, she spots Eamon and makes her way over. Though he wants her to sit next to him, to watch her sit as she maneuvers her dress properly to cover her legs, he stands. *Gentlemanly*, he thinks.

They both say "hey."

"Just in time for the jump," he says.

"Hold on."

She walks off and gets two Stellas out of the cooler next to the grill. She opens them on the gargoyle attached to the side of Dave's house for just such purposes.

"Sorry. I needed this."

Eamon nods.

"What did you bring?"

"Grape tomatoes. From my garden."

Out of a goddamned painting, Eamon thinks. She hands him one, and it's so sweet that Eamon forgets what he's eating for a moment. He thinks, *This would make a weird but nice perfume.*

"They're so sweet," he says. "Almost like candy."

"I know. Aren't they great?"

"Almost too great."

"Yeah. I didn't know vegetables could taste like candy."

"The tomato is a fruit," Eamon says.

"I know. Technically. But come on. Who really thinks tomatoes are fruits?"

Dave arrives.

"Here it comes," he says.

"This better own up," says Rachael.

"It will," says Dave. "Where's your boytoy? Couldn't stomach it?"

"He had to work. Not like us. He has to work for a living."

"He sucks. His loss."

Dave runs off and circles everyone in the backyard, a one-man publicity machine for his sad little stunt. Eamon feels sick. Of course Rachael has a boyfriend. The thought hadn't even occurred to him. He feels like a new law has just been put in place, like a cruel dictator has just mandated it illegal to sleep at night. His life was one way, and now it's another. *Rachael the detective*, he thinks, *would have found this information right away. She's brilliant.*

"OK everyone, on this, my 38th year, I want to thank you all for sharing it with me," Dave is speaking from his roof, one foot on a shingle, one on the gutter. He tosses his Cubs cap to the ground for effect. "As you all know, this is tradition. So long as I remain unharmed, so I remain a man in my youth, in my prime, and in my glory. I want to thank my lovely wife for indulging me in this, though in accordance with tradition she is not joining us here today because the 18-foot drop makes her a little nervous. I don't blame her. Kids, don't try this at home. You don't need to check in on your youth. And I know in my heart that I don't need to check on mine. But here it is. My annual plunge. Semper fi!"

Dave, falling, is a sight. His red hair lifts off his head like grass underwater. His shirt rises and belly fat announces itself with a white sheen. His shorts ride up, too, folding in waves to reveal freckled legs. When he hits the ground—in the slow motion brains reel through such events—his feet slap against the lawn. His ass follows shortly thereafter, his thighs meeting his calves with a farting sound and his butt colliding with his heels. He stumbles back, pushes with his feet, hits his head on the grill, and tumbles onto his side. The people in the backyard don't know whether to laugh or to run to his aid. He continues to roll. There's too much movement in him, and he collides with the cooler, finally bringing him to a stop. It's not the descent of aging, it would seem, it's the momentum.

Dave is slow to rise. He takes two hesitant steps forward, raises his arms wide, and screams, "Victory!" Everyone screams in response, even though it's obvious he's limping badly off his right leg, even though it's obvious the blood pouring from the side of his head is from a wound that will need stitching, and even though it's not obvious at all who or what this particular triumph trumped. Eamon cups his hands to clap a hollow, echoing applause.

Rachael hands Eamon another tomato, which tastes even sweeter, which is to say, tastes even worse.

On the train ride home, he is trapped within the bay of doors, squeezed behind a crowd of baseball fans smelling of booze and sunscreen. He can hear Dr. Dre and Snoop Dogg through the headphones of the woman behind him. The long hair of the woman to his left scratches his forearm, but there is nowhere else for him to put it. *Not if you were the last woman on Earth*, Eamon transmits to the back of the woman's head. *Ditto*, the back of her head responds.

On Monday, Eamon types the following e-mail to himself:

```
Date: Mon, 18 Sep 2006 09:34:12 (-0700)
From: Epeterson@hdcapital.com
To: aymon@hotmail.com
Subject: No more kidding yourself

forget it. failure has come for you and you have no
answer for it. you're not the type to continue on!
```

A half hour later, he checks his e-mail and reads this one over and over again. The Big Lie Theory, Eamon thinks. Eventually, this will be true. Clicking back to the Index page, he sees another e-mail emerge. According to the time stamp, he wrote it while he was filing.

```
Date: Mon, 18 Sep 2006 10:06:26 (-0700)
From: Epeterson@hdcapital.com
To: aymon@hotmail.com
Subject: Be rash-onal!

Dude, stop being so hard on yourself. Pick yourself
up and get back out there. She wants it, you just
have to let her know. You're the man!
```

Eamon writes back: Stop writing me. He stares at his work e-mail window, watches as it appears at the top of the list of new e-mails, waits for it to pale, signifying it's been read.

Unperturbed by the obvious frightening nature of these e-mails, of what they say about the status of his mental health, about a potentially fractured psyche, Eamon considers the Other Him as he cleans off his desk, filing every bit of manila information. Who is this Other Eamon? Where does all of this confidence come from? Why is he so much clearer in his thinking? Why is it that his crazy side–the piece of him that emerges when he loses time–gets to have his shit together while Eamon wallows in his ineffectual wooing?

Eamon skips lunch. He retires to the back of the library, opens the last file drawer slightly, and curls up on the floor, awash in ambivalence over this Other Eamon. There's potential there. At least a part of him is trying to improve. He need only combine the two.

It takes several rings of the bell to awaken Eamon. His eyes open on the beige wall. His mouth tastes like cheese. *Is this the taste of sleep, or a leftover from another me?* The bell rings again.

"Dude! Are you back there?"

"Just finishing up the filing!"

Eamon kicks the drawer shut.

"Dude, I'm sorry, I was just fucking with you."

Dave is standing there, hands on the counter. He looks different. Lopsided. As Eamon approaches, he notices that his boss's hair is thinner on the right side. The doctors had to clip it to stitch the wound. He doesn't mention it.

"What are you talking about?"

"The e-mails. We were just fucking around. Me and the IT guys."

At Hopedale Capital, Dave tells him, e-mailing oneself throws up all kinds of red flags. "Company secrets, dude." An employee repeatedly e-mailing himself could be an indication that he has files he wants to distribute elsewhere. When the IT guys brought it to Dave's attention, and he saw the Rachael Morneau messages, he decided to join in the fun.

"But you got me, man. The tone of that last e-mail made me feel a little guilty. I didn't mean anything by it."

Eamon nods and Dave leaves. Eamon wonders if there's ever been anyone who mourned the death of a split personality. Now he knows that confidence is nowhere within him; it's in Dave, recharged every year in a fall from a roof. Eamon turns his web browser to assexprass.com, large mounds of naked flesh rising to the fore of his laptop screen. *Fuck it*, Eamon thinks. *If I'm going to be monitored at work, I might as well do something worth monitoring.* At 5 o'clock, Eamon takes the last file from his counter, slips it into his messenger bag, and exits.

Eamon sips a beer at the Exchequer bar. He knows Gilbert Madden is here, in the back room, but he's not ready to see him yet. Eamon is wondering if he can fracture his own psyche, if he can force a new him, one that will draw a curtain around the current Eamon and do what the current version is too afraid to do. A blow to the head, an emotional shock, these things could do the trick. Despite Dave's betrayal, the ethical breach Eamon contemplates is not easily undertaken. There is the salary, the naps, and Rachael to consider. After four beers, Eamon thinks, *Get real.*

He makes his way to the back of Exchequer. It's one of those Chicago bars with multiple back and side rooms, passing through them is like walking through a Japanese mausoleum, Eamon thinks, not sure what he means by it. He sees Gilbert Madden immediately. Of course it's him. His head is bald in a way that makes aging seem fashionable. He has on the nicest suit Eamon has ever seen. It's silk, but Eamon still wonders what animals had to be killed to make a suit that nice. Cufflinks sparkle from its dark sleeves like rocks in an aquarium.

"Gil," he says.

"Eamon."

"I appreciate your time."

Sitting across from Gilbert Madden, Eamon feels powerless. This man, a criminal through and through and yet as successful a man as Eamon has encountered, seems like a distant relative. It's the same feeling he remembers from his childhood, when he'd run to any man with pants the same color as his father's and cling to his knees, only to look up and see a strange face smiling back at him, a mistaken intimacy that couldn't be erased.

Gilbert Madden orders Eamon a whiskey and soda. Eamon puts his hand over the glass so he's not tempted to drink it. Gilbert Madden begins to talk about his past, how in high school he never took life seriously, and when he graduated he worked for his uncle as a carpet layer. Eamon makes it a point not to listen. He doesn't want to imagine Gil as anything other than a successful, international playboy. He doesn't want to envision Gil as scrawny, as laying carpet, as mortal.

"Eventually, I'd made a lot of money," says Gil. "Owned the business."

Eamon wishes he didn't have to listen to people narrate their own stories. He wants to tell Gil who he is. *You were an orphan who learned the logic of the streets early. By 16, you'd made your name as a jewelry thief. The only kind of carpet you laid was red, see.*

"People call them blood diamonds, but I think a sparkle is a sparkle," says Gil. This is more like it.

"I have what you want," says Eamon.

"But we haven't even discussed the terms."

Eamon already knows the terms. He'll get a sum of money, in cash, that will make loyalty to Hopedale an absurd notion, a laughable ethic held over from an Eamon past. But really, by handing over all of this corporate intelligence, he'll be buying into the story of Gil. His story of Gil: The man who can bring women and Africa to their knees.

Gil and Eamon slide envelopes across the table to each other like complementary pistons. A diner at the table two over from them—a man of astonishingly shadowy cheeks—stands and plucks Eamon's envelope from the table. This is more like it!

"How many of the people in this restaurant right now work for you, Gil?"

"Just Charlie."

Eamon believes he's lying, scans the room for other worker bees, is delighted he can't pick any out. *They're too good*, he thinks.

"Time for you to go, Eamon."

Eamon smiles and nods. He stuffs his envelope of cash into his messenger bag and turns to leave. Shakes Gil's hand.

And as he's leaving, Gil says something to Eamon, something that he wants Eamon to hear, but Eamon doesn't listen to it. He bounces it from his brain. He looks around the room and imagines that all of the diners and drinkers are keeping a special eye on him. Gil is still speaking. Eamon muffles it before it reaches his ears.

But what Gil is saying is: "Nothing went on here tonight. Nothing special about a guy trying to live his life. Nothing special at all."

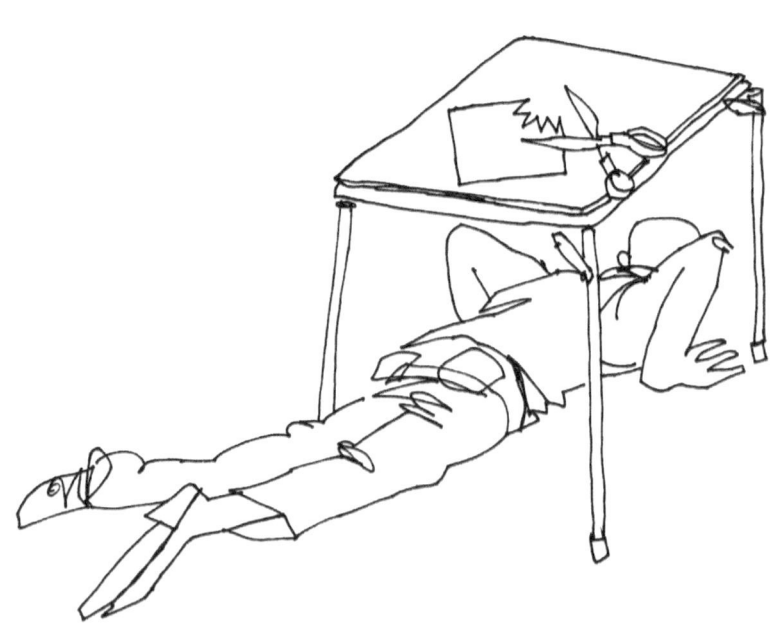

TRUE HERO

I put on my costume and went to the party. I wasn't invited, but I went anyway.

The party was a long walk from my apartment. I should have taken the bus, but it wasn't that cold inside my costume and, besides, I didn't have any pockets that could hold my bus pass. It took 75 minutes to walk there.

I could tell it was going to be a good one because everyone there was in costume. I hate the party libertarians who claim they shouldn't have to wear a costume if they don't want to. They're as annoying at parties as actual libertarians.

I had arrived earlier than planned. A half hour in, I still hadn't talked to anyone. It was part of my costume.

My concept: a True Hero; a robotic force for good in a future where there is only evil and injustice. I started building the liner in July 2004, the week after the last party. I went online to an S&M warehouse and bought a lycra suit a size smaller than I really am. I planned on skinnying my gut, which, a year later, is heavily bolded on my list of unaccomplished goals. I sashed several slim belts across the liner and connected rappelling hooks, also purchased online, to each in various locations. Then, I went to work on the inner shell.

The couple who threw the party was dressed as foreign gods. It wasn't immediately clear to me which mythology had spawned them, as the guy was encased in chafing green body paint and haphazard white and gold bed sheets. Likewise the lady of the house wore a black wig with hair as thick as snakes. Her skin was lacquered with the same Crayola-brand skin toner, though she was a plasticky yellow. Her body paint showed none of her partner's flaking, proving it's sometimes true that ladies are too demure to sweat.

If I'd wished to speak, my first question would have been, "What manner of gods are the two of you?" And my second: "Who throws a party to turn themselves into gods?" The answer: "Pretty much everybody." The truth of the matter: I was angry I hadn't thought of the whole setup first.

A guy with a large hairdo that, were it curly would be called an afro, manned the turntables. He was dressed, like all DJs at costume parties, as a robot. His name was Cliff or Clyde or some other name that made me wonder if he was born to play the role he was in tonight. He had a lazy eye. I was fascinated by this lazy-eyed robot. The eye is such an important part of robot iconography—for locking in on targets, for scanning terrains. It's one of the main signifiers that the metal man is different from the flesh. When you look into the eyes of a robot, you don't even bother searching for a soul. All you'll get is a synthetic glow. With the reason I was there still nowhere in sight, for me the party centered on him.

The lady host approached, staring at the robot playing a mash-up of The Rolling Stones and Ginuwine, and asked, "Hey, have we met?" I returned her look, but as she couldn't see my face behind the mask, she couldn't know who I was. "Who is that in there?" she asked. I didn't respond.

"Oh OK, you're one of those guys who isn't going to talk in his costume," she said. "That's funny for a little while, but it's going to get creepy real fast." She left me and my desperate DJ alone. He shrugged and put on another record.

The inner shell of my costume was made of a foam rubber. The hooks from the lycra suit slide easily through the slits I cut in the industrial fiber. This rubber was supposed to be breathable, but on the walk over here I could feel my sweat coat me like petroleum. I should have known better.

I wandered the party for some time, and none of the guests could guess at who or what I was, nor why I was there. I suppose if there were a trained psychologist at the party we could have drawn some conclusions by what people saw in me. A cute girl dressed as Margot Tenenbaum told me she thought I was a walking vending machine. Another girl in the same costume told me I was a post-apocalyptic cupid. I avoided her for the rest of the night.

Jesse, a guy I had probably met before, tried his hand. There was no way to avoid being bored by his guesses. He ventured Voltron, Power Ranger, Robocop and Big Brother before finally giving up. He was dressed as Saddam Hussein, but without a mustache and without pants. What should have been a red beret was yellow and he was drinking a 40 oz. of Olde English with half a lemon jammed down the neck. "You want to know what I am?" he asked. I shook my head and walked away. That knowledge wasn't going to get me anywhere.

The host of the party, the green guy who was ruining his bed sheets with his kindergarten body paint, appeared. I retreated back to the living room and looked longingly at a bowl of chips standing next to some salsa. There was no way to get anything into my mask. "Hey man, I'm Zach," he said. He extended his hand but I didn't return his good favor. He mistook it for part of the costume. "Listen, your costume is amazing. Seriously. I love it."

I stood still.

"My fiancée, she's the one in the yellow paint, you know, Wadjet, the protective serpent goddess of Lower Egypt," he said. I nodded. "She just gets a little skittish when she doesn't know everyone at the party. And I get the, uh, the no-talking thing. So, if I know you, just nod, and we'll be cool."

I was still waiting, not ready to go home yet, so I nodded.

The outer shell of the True Hero prototype, of course, took the most time to prepare. I took plaster casts of various parts of my body and constructed cardboard and leather body plates for my armor. I painted laser decals on my shoulders, pelvis and knees. Electronics marked the sides of my torso, flanking a red light in the center. I constructed my mask from an old bike helmet and papier-mâché using shredded cardboard. I left the gun I made at home, thinking it looked too fake, but I carried a store-bought plastic machete. None of this interested me. The only essential element was the box just above my heart, colored brass.

I resumed my position by the lazy-eyed robot DJ. The speakers set up near his station made conversation difficult, and I figured I would be left alone by default. He was now deep in argument with a man dressed as Jesus but wearing blackface.

"I have over a million mp3s!" shouted the DJ in a quiet moment of a song. "Imagine that. Over a million mp3s! You can't even conceive of that!" Blackface Jesus was just shaking his head and telling the DJ that, no matter how many mp3s he had, he was still an asshole. You could count the number of drinks each man had downed by the degree to which he took himself seriously. "I will arm-wrestle you," the DJ offered. Blackface Jesus assented and turned toward me.

"Who are you supposed to be?" I shrugged my shoulders. I drew comfort from the failure of a man dressed as this to identify me. Never had there been an outsider like me.

The outer shell of the costume was held to the foam rubber through the rappelling hooks. They slid out from the lycra like tentacles, clinging to my second layer of remove. The setup was genius. I moved as easily as I would in five pair of pants, which is better than you'd think.

Hungry and thirsty, I searched out a solution. There was little room in my mask for any sort of entry. Shortly after I figured out how to maneuver a straw into my mouth, I saw her. It was only her back, but it was enough. The top of her head was at shoulder-height with the two guys facing her and her hair was darker than I remembered; a shade too dark to remember. Her green dress with a ginger trim was from a decade long past, just like her, from a time when a woman only had one dress so lovely.

I couldn't hear what she was saying to the tall men around her, a couple of guys dressed as '80s athletes in headbands, wristbands, half-shirts and crotch-hugging short shorts. I hated them like I hated the '80s.

I stuck close to the lazy-eyed robot DJ who, now back at his station, was like everyone at the party: He regarded me as furniture. She finished her conversation with the guys, and they lumbered to the keg. She turned and it was then that I saw she was wearing a mask I had made for her. Last year.

I made her the mask of plaster of Paris and a fancy, expensive glaze I bought at the craft store. It felt like liquid DNA, the way it made the mask so human. She said she wanted us to look like we were at the last party on the Lusitania. Her features were already so fine; I was at a loss as to how to make her look more regal, so I made her look older, lines near her eyes from a life spent laughing. I curled the front of her hair the way she always talked about training it. She had a small burgundy birthmark on her right cheek, a wonderful lily pad along her jaw line. When she saw that I had painted it on her mask, we kissed.

She flitted over to the keg, exchanged an awkward smile with the '80s athletes, acknowledging that they had nothing left to say to each other. Her back was to me again and I could relax. I hung tight near Robot DJ and Blackface Jesus, who at that point had alienated everyone at the party with their weird acts of bravado. They let me stand with them because I wasn't disruptive, and three looked more like a party than two. We were quite a trinity, innately flawed but thinking ourselves perfect. No one took a picture of us.

She let a guy dressed as Edward Penishands fill her cup from the tap. I almost interrupted, a rare moment of guts, but I knew that sort of humor never worked on her. She quickly disengaged from Penishands' stare and turned toward me. She looked straight into the red eyes of my mask and flinched. She hastened toward me, but I couldn't get a read on her emotion behind her mask. I was sure she knew it was me, and I crossed my right hand over my chest to touch the brass box above my heart.

She stopped three feet away and said, "Is that you in there?" I froze. Despite all of my preparations, I had planned no response. She stepped even closer, put her hand against the light in my torso and said, "Nod if it's you." She had to have known for sure to put it so bluntly. I shrugged my shoulders. Behind the three layers that made up my costume, all I wanted was to feel her hand.

She spun and hooked a quick arm around a passing Wadjet, the protective serpent goddess of Lower Egypt, whose jaundiced, sweaty skin was now flaking in dandruff piles around her. The two confabbed, and I knew there was nothing Wadjet could say about me that would confirm or deny my identity. I had few moments left for courage.

She and Wadjet spoke in clipped whispers, spinning the situation before them into possible worst-case scenarios. I decided to pretend like I was friends with Blackface Jesus and Robot DJ, so I nodded to the music. The helmet was heavy and I was way offbeat.

"What are you supposed to be anyway?" said Blackface Jesus, through with yet another argument with the Robot DJ, this one about who could complete more consecutive chin-ups. I kept up my clumsy head nod.

"Leave him alone," said the DJ. "This guy's cool. He hasn't

spoken to anyone all night. You could learn something from him."
And the two of them began an argument about who was the better
conversationalist. I should have, as soon as I saw her, gone right
over to her and plucked the box from my chest and handed it to
her. But that wasn't as easy as standing there.

She and Wadjet steeled themselves for an upcoming
confrontation. I watched as they snarled and shivered. She didn't
want to approach me again, but she didn't want Wadjet to do it
alone. The green god came over and, once updated, mouthed,
"No way," before the classless idiot looked me over. Another guy,
someone I hadn't yet seen and who was still wearing a jacket
walked over to her with his back to me. When she saw him, she
smiled and crumpled and buried her head in his chest.

*The brass box on the left of my chest took a great deal of time to
make. I stole a square bin from outside a men's clothing store, the
kind used to preserve ties for fancy weddings. I stripped the cloth on
the outside and replaced it with brass-colored contact paper. Inside
the box was a message for her, written in a careful cursive on a long,
thin strip of paper and rolled into a scroll.*

The two gods scurried to be the first to update the new arrival
on the situation. I heard someone say the words "ex-boyfriend" and
"creepy." It hurt like insults hadn't hurt since I was a kid. I thought,
"I'm the only true hero who would follow your shadow."

I looked at Jesus and the Robot so I wouldn't have to watch,
and when I looked back again, her boyfriend was striding toward
me. He wore no costume, but clung to his face was my counterpart,
the mask I had made for my role in the Lusitania couple. I said my

first word of the night, and it was, "Jesus." Blackface Jesus turned and said, "Excuse me?"

Her Lusitania mask had taken me hours to mold, plaster and paint. But I didn't know what to do with my face, so I sloppily crafted a generic plaster mask. It was the perfect metaphor for our time together.

Before her boyfriend grabbed me by my cardboard shoulders and shoved me into the wall, I was able to remove the brass box. I held it in my hand like a fossil—old news that only still held interest for me. Her boyfriend, looking gallant in my old featureless mask, sunk a hand through the torso of my costume and came back with a fistful of foam rubber. I caved. He and the green god and probably one of the '80s athletes grabbed me and I passed by her, three feet away, as they threw me out the front door. My costume tore in the most embarrassing places, leaving just a lycra suit tight around my ass and my middle. My mask was ruined, but I left it on as I made my way to the sidewalk.

On the walk home, I became convinced that—just as I was being scrummed out the front—I had heard a loud thud against the doorframe. It must have been someone throwing the brass box after me. And before I went over the first-floor porch railing, I believed I had heard her ask them to stop. She never came outside to see if I was OK, so it was likely my imagination. But I hoped she was inside, opening that brass box. I imagined her unfurling the scroll until it delicately touched her toes, and reading from the message carefully written on that thin paper, making her smile. And I prayed that it wasn't just another thing she would wrap around her new boyfriend and call his.

NOT EVEN THE ZOOKEEPER CAN KEEP CONTROL

The zoo acquired a man-eating wolf. It was a public relations stunt, because too many passive animals at the zoo have recently died: an elephant, two giraffes and a manatee. Peaceable animals that are supposed to outlive humans. The zoo board acquired the man-eating wolf to reverse its karma and maybe to show it has a sense of humor. The zoo did not feed the wolf humans, but rather mice. They permitted him to chew on the old bones of dead prisoners. He seemed to like it.

Tourists went to the zoo and watched it from behind bulletproof glass. The wolf salivated at the sight of the onlookers, drool lolling from his jaws and, on occasion, he pointed at the most frightened as if ordering at a deli.

Attendance at the zoo was up.

Within a week, the zoo lost the man-eating wolf. It happened four days ago and the newspapers have to at least pretend to be serious. The best headline pun the news can come up with is off the Michael J. Fox movie: "Mean Wolf."

"Is that the best they can do?" I ask you. You, sitting most often on the futon and reading the newspapers, feet on the coffee table. You ignore me. I sit down beside you and hand you a glass of orange juice. The air around you is hot like you just came out of the dryer. It's been days since we've touched.

The town is not handling well the news of the on-the-loose man-eating wolf. It's not so much the news, but the man eating. There was a public meeting the other day at the Second Congregational Church. The people of the town asked the zoo board of commissioners, "Why the fuck did you bring a man-eating wolf to our town?" And the zoo board of commissioners said, "Well, who the fuck let the man-eating wolf out, because it wasn't us?" And then, because the public meeting happened in a church, everyone in the church, in unison, asked, "Why the fuck did god make a man-eating wolf?"

"I think I love this wolf," you say. It has been eight days since the wolf's escape and 35 people have turned up missing or as piles of bones. The math doesn't add up.

"How could you love something so destructive?" I ask.

"Because this wolf doesn't care if your heart is whole or not," you say. "It tastes just the same."

The air around you is cold like you've just been reanimated. You suggest making love, but now I'm too afraid.

I find the zookeeper in Cove Park, crouched behind a bush, not too far from the gazebo. He looks beaten. His brown and gold uniform is torn and his eyes are so bloodshot I wonder if they could shoot lasers.

"Why are you hiding here?" I ask. It's nighttime. Neither of us should be here.

"I'm trying to get my wolf back," he says. He reaches below the bush and pulls out a mammoth harpoon, the kind usually rigged to a tall ship.

"Why not just use a gun?" I ask.

"I don't have a permit," he says, as though I've wounded him. It occurs to me that the harpoon may have been stolen.

"I don't think people expect you to catch the wolf yourself," I say. "I don't know if they're blaming you anymore."

"Who are they blaming, then?"

"Right now it looks like God," I say.

"Yeah, that'll never last," he says, and sprints across the park, still in a crouch, as if bullets are tearing the air above his head, or his back has been broken. In the distance, we both hear a wolf howl, and the zookeeper swings and squirms, straightens up and trips over the roots of a tree. The harpoon fires and the spear bounces with an unsharpened thud against the tree trunk. The thing is plastic. Watching the zookeeper groan on the ground next to his toy harpoon is so painful I laugh.

Ten days of the man-eating wolf rampage and some 233 people have been killed. How is this possible? Another meeting is called at the church. I go because who wouldn't go.

The high school principal, trying to pass himself off as a preacher, is at the helm this time. The zoo board is there, in the pews, as is everyone else that I've ever seen in the town, except for you and the zookeeper. Our town is now small enough to fit everyone in these pews.

"Man-eating wolves are not the problem," the principal says.

"The fact that none of us can learn from our mistakes is the problem."

The members of the zoo board shout hallelujahs, but they are the only ones.

"I for one think the wolf is teaching us a lesson," the principal says. "Maybe we need this wolf to thin the herd."

Even the zoo board is a little wary of praising that.

"I'm confused," I say, because no one else would. "If it's only one wolf, why are there 233 dead and more missing?"

The principal glares at me from atop the altar. He menaces.

"No one in the room," he bellows. "No one in the room get to know this man! Don't get close to him, because I'm sure he will pretty soon be eaten!"

I leave the church right away, because I am afraid the principal is able to summon the man-eating wolf at will and the beast will burst through the church doors and devour me, bones and all. But even if that isn't the case, I would have left anyway, because what the principal said just wasn't cool.

I take a walk in the park, hoping to find the zookeeper again. It isn't that hard—he's back behind the bush with his plastic harpoon and tattered uniform. He looks even worse for the wear.

"Did you go to the meeting?" he asks.

I hunker beside him, behind the bush. I realize he's not alone back there. There's a woman with him. She's wild-eyed and smiling at me like I should know her. I notice that the zookeeper has his hand down her pants.

"It's a basic need," he tells me.

"You should be concentrating," I tell him.

"Don't judge," he says. "What did they say about me, at the meeting, at church?"

"Everyone's counting on you to find the wolf," I say. I walk away, leaving him there, shaking.

You won't come back with me to the gazebo. You want to stay in the house. You say you've heard enough about the wolf and it's time we started talking about something else. I try to tell you about the principal, how he said that the wolf would eat me, and that no one should get close to me. You laugh. A breeze blows through like something is leaving the room. You say you can hear the ocean, even though there's nothing but pavement outside our window.

Wolf cries are regular now. I hear them in mono. No one has actually seen the wolf since it escaped, but it's there. On my way to the church I steal some new sneakers. I've never stolen anything of value, but no one is working the store anymore, and I feel like running shoes are a good idea.

I walk through the center of town, trying to find the source of the howls, but the wolf is fast and I am slow. I make my way to the church, but nothing is happening yet. Bones are piling and sprawling in the streets and alleys, now that even the street cleaners are gone. Legions of buzzards circle above. The sky has become a dismal fishbowl. The buzzards rarely swoop. The bones are always picked clean, which makes me wonder about the nature of this wolf. If the wolf is so insatiable, would he not take the heart and move on for more, his taste and hunger wrapping into one? If this wolf were passionate, he wouldn't nitpick.

I circle back to the church and get in just in time, just as the doors are being bolted shut. Inside people are drinking cocoa and eating goldfish crackers out of small snack bags. We look like refugees. No one has anything left to say. The principal is here, but he only glares at me, as if he's disappointed he couldn't summon the wolf to eat me. When it becomes clear no one has any new insight, we file out, silently.

I walk around Cove Park, don't go directly to the bush by the gazebo, where I'm sure the zookeeper is still awaiting his fate. I pass by hedgerow after hedgerow, rose bushes and chainlink fences. I'm looking for prints. Or shit. One would think that a huge, man-eating wolf would have to leave huge prints or man-eating shits behind. I hear a wolf bay again, a lone voice in harmony with itself.

There's the zookeeper, lying on his side.

"I haven't slept in days," he says.

"Neither have I."

"If I don't find this wolf soon, it's going to kill me the old-fashioned way," he says.

The zookeeper and I both fall silent. I can hear both of our heartbeats, mine less regular than his, or vice versa. I think about what you said, about a heart being of the same quality when stripped of its mystical properties. But then, why hasn't the wolf come for the zookeeper, or for me? Another howl and his heartbeat is like radio static. I pick up his harpoon and follow the sound. The zookeeper wants to follow me—I know he does—but he's in no condition.

I ditch the harpoon in a dumpster and walk the edges of town. The wolf is moving in a circle, ever closing. I hear his howl so deeply it's as if it's coming from my throat. I wonder why no one has thought of this before, to just follow the sound of the beast and snuff it where it stands. Or maybe they have, and that's why we haven't seen them again.

I see it. I know you don't want to hear what it looks like. You hoped that it wasn't going to make an appearance in this story, but I'm going to tell you anyway. It's disappointing. It's small. Its jaws are tight and its muscles lean, but from this angle it looks no more dangerous than a house pet. It looks comfortable, cozy. Up close its bays are so loud that I hear them muffled, like I'm underwater. Its fur is the same brown of the zookeeper's uniform. You wouldn't believe it, but I can feel my heart stop when it turns to look at me. It makes me wonder if it really eats men, or if it simply scares them to death.

But no, it definitely eats men, because it's running after me, growling. The spit flying from its mouth skips on the pavement like gravel. I sprint in my new shoes, the soles squeaking. The wolf is behind me, I know it. I trip on something. I think it must be a root, or a crack in the sidewalk. But I realize it's a pile of bones. For some reason, these bones remind me of you. Of course they aren't your bones, because you're still here. But as I roll onto my side, staring at the crystallized end of a dismembered joint, I wonder if it's yours. And when the wolf, bearing down behind me, finally reaches for my chest, I wonder if my heart will taste different from yours.

ONE VALVE OPENS

At Oak Park-River Forest High School, Julius is dope. He is a poetry stud. When the Poetry Slam Club threw its annual competition his junior year, he took the stage just prior to guest judge and performer Reg E. Gaines and, after he won, girls and even some guys told him he was as good as Reg. He believed them, and he continued writing.

Now, as he prepares for his senior slam, his journalism class is visited by a young reporter from the local paper. The reporter is white, clean-cut, his clothes hinting—through slight tears in sneakers and worn blue-collar work pants on a Casual Friday—at a punk-rock persona in his private life. Julius is not sure what to make of this young reporter who has come to develop a page in the paper with high school students. To some extent, Julius would like his poetry published, but he is skeptical of the reporter's casual punk-rock sensibility, which means he is hiding something, that he is beholden to others. He may try to change the poem.

The reporter promises to publish as is or not at all, but Julius is still hesitant. The reporter, not knowing the school scuttlebutt, thinks nothing of asking Julius's friend John if he has anything he would like to submit. In his eyes, the two friends are equally skilled poets. Julius immediately assents.

Within a few weeks, Julius and the punk-rock reporter hash out a deal where he works with the reporter on an essay about black life in a suburban high school. In return, the reporter looks the other way while Julius checks his fantasy baseball statistics or occasionally works on a new poem about a girl. When the reporter and John discuss hip-hop and John calls out during class, "Jules! Dude listens to Wordsworth," Julius acts unimpressed.

While the reporter works with Julius on his essay he also helps a white girl in the class write about a friend who died of a heroin overdose last summer. The girl is pretty and filled out in the hips and Julius suspects the reporter of exploiting her story. He begins to wonder about whether the reporter is exploiting him like he is the girl.

———

Julius and Ayana, the girl in the new poem, are in the middle of a break-up. Ayana says Julius is too full of himself. She does not say, "You think you all that," or "Y'all just a playa," or "Why you be like that," which are direct quotes from the girls in his previous break-up poems. Julius wonders how he got the impression that's how people talk to each other.

Ayana tells him she thinks he is selfish and that between college applications, working at night and seeing her friends before she leaves for school, she doesn't want to work at keeping him happy. Julius wonders why she looks more beautiful to him now than when they were happy. Her hair is the color of sun-kissed fruit, her skin rocking chair brown, her breath a silent morning. He thinks this again and again when he cries to himself at night. When he picks up the love poem again, he ends it with the girl saying, "I ain't tryin' to be a hatah, but I'll see yo' ass latah." The reporter raises no objections to the poem's conclusion—actually puts his fist out to be knocked by Julius's knuckles—raising Julius's suspicions to a fever pitch.

———·•·———

Julius tells his family—in the kitchen while his mother cooks and his little brother Willie sets the table—that he is to have a poem published in the newspaper.

"What's this one about?" she asks, watching carefully as she stirs vegetables in a fragrant pot.

"About how love doesn't exist," he says.

His mother laughs, a high-pitched laugh that Willie and Julius call "the dog whistle."

"So it's about Ayana, then."

Julius tersely denies it. Willie, 12 years old and just beginning to chase girls in seventh grade, does a bizarre little hula dance and sways his head back and forth like a metronome, singing "Oh Ayana, Oh Ayana," giving her name sing-song peaks and valleys. Julius doesn't react because tonight is the one night of the week his mother is home from work for supper. He grabs a pen from a drawer below the kitchen counter and draws an "X" on the back of his hand. It is to remind him to beat Willie for this dance tomorrow.

Their apartment on the southeast side of town is only three blocks from where crews dig up Barrie Park, excavating mountains of soil after several neighbors contracted cancer. There are carcinogenic remnants in the soil from an old gas plant that once occupied the same site. Everyone within a block of the park was paid to move while crews labor within a giant tent that now covers the park like an airplane hangar. It is a billion-dollar project. Looking out the window at the tent, Julius wonders whether he would rather take his chances with cancer in the park, or bullets and drugs two blocks east, in Austin. When he was a toddler, before his mother left his father and took the Oak Park apartment, he lived there. His memories of that time are now like dreams, foggy and buried deep somewhere in the bottom of his stomach. He thinks he would send Willie, who has fallen asleep in the bed next to him, to the cancerous park every day before he let him cross Austin Boulevard. He does not write a poem about these feelings.

In school, his classmates all hang over copies of the newspaper. Julius doesn't know whether they are reading his poem or the heroin girl's story, but soon his friends and a few people he doesn't know approach him, pat his back, shake his hand, knock his fist. John asks if Ayana has seen it yet—everyone knows it's about her— but Julius doesn't know because it's been five days since he has spoken with her. He saw her that morning near the tennis courts, paper in hand, but moved stealthily away.

"No, man," is all he says.

John goes back to work on a poem the slam team he started with Julius—tentatively named Da Trax—will perform at the school's slam in three weeks. John reads aloud part of what he has written, a reaction to a store owner asking him if he stole something. The end of his part rhymes "angel's wings" with "Doctor King."

At that point, John wants Julius to take over because Julius's last name is King, and the crowd—who know well his legend—will go wild. Julius just puts his head on his desk and thinks of how he would rather not write again.

———•◦•———

That Friday, the casually punk-rock reporter returns to the room bearing a stack of papers for the students. He is wearing low-top Chuck Taylor All-Stars and there are pins on his bag for bands with names Julius doesn't recognize, but nearly all begin with "The."

He takes Julius into the computer room and asks him if he's had much reaction to the poem. Everyone at the paper, it seems, liked it.

"Yeah, a few people said some things," Julius says. He doesn't know why he feels ashamed in front of the reporter. He doesn't know why he wants to get out of the room as quickly as possible. But the reporter wants to talk; but he says "shoot the shit" because the teacher is in the other room and the reporter cares little about the school's honor code. He asks Julius if he's getting ready for the school slam. Julius, feeling thin and unlike himself around the reporter, says he'll get ready when he's ready.

"You cover that Barrie Park story?" Julius asks.

The reporter says he does, looking at Julius as if he just asked a personal question in a job interview.

"Tell me about it," Julius says, and puts his head on the desk. Without hesitation, the reporter talks about excavation and remediation, carcinogens and soil sampling, air tests and coal gas manufacturing. Julius keeps his head down, but the reporter doesn't take it as a sign of boredom. There is a passion that raises the reporter's voice an octave higher.

At Da Trax's fifth rehearsal, everyone on the team has their part ready, except for Julius. He has begun working on it, but is skeptical of reading aloud the first draft. He is protective of his works in progress. To expose them early is to water them down.

Da Trax consists of six poets: Julius, John, Damian, Malcolm, Peter and Xavier, who insists on being known as X Spot when he performs his poetry. Every member of Da Trax is black, something Julius and John required from the beginning and were able to sustain, despite the desire of the other original three to include an Asian kid named Danny. Allowing Xavier as the sixth member was the compromise to which Julius and John eventually relented.

Julius is the anchor. Xavier will start out the poem because, as ridiculous as he is to Julius, he possesses the most energy. Julius thinks his rhymes are too close to brag-rap to be considered poetry, but the way Xavier says them, like he's squeezing them from the back of his sinuses, is odd and charismatic. Each member presents his own style, with John's part culminating in the most confrontational moment of the poem. Julius will pick it up from there. And from there, he thinks, he will go in a new direction.

The reporter and Julius have a half-hour meeting scheduled to discuss his essay about black suburban student life. Julius has just come from lunch, where he accidentally bumped into Ayana, her eyes cold, lips sealed. He said, "Whassup," and reached out to her, but she shook her head and huffed, leaving him standing there without saying anything. Someone behind Julius said, "Damn," but he didn't turn around.

The reporter, dressed in business attire, wants to know how the essay is coming. At this point, the reporter looks as comfortable in a tie as he does in his other clothes, so much so that Julius wonders which one is the disguise.

Julius says he has too much to do.

"You can't work on more than one thing at once?" the reporter asks, and Julius thinks he is trying to be young and tough with him.

"Why's it gotta be about being a black student?" Julius says. "Why's being a black student any different than being just a student? Why can't I just write an essay about being a student, whether I'm black or not?"

"Write what you want," the reporter says. "If you really think there's no difference between your experience and the dozen white kids writing essays for the student paper, then write the same thing."

Julius thinks he is being set up.

That night at home, Julius sits against the wall that serves as his bed's headboard, his pillow and one from Willie's bed propping his back. Willie has slept without a pillow ever since he saw a film on the Discovery Channel about Yogis in India. Julius caught Willie wearing his mother's nightgown one night, his head and arm together through the neck of the blue-starred gown, a poor approximation of an Indian dhoti. Rather than looking like Gandhi, Julius thought, Willie looked like Martin Lawrence's Sheneneh character. At first, he thought it was something he should report to his mother, but Willie was stoic in his response to being caught.

"Yogis have no worries," he said, and Julius laughed for hours at his little brother's gravitas.

Julius has two notebooks, one in his lap, another on the bed beside him. The one in his lap is for the essay, and he scribbles intently within the margins, feeling strong about the form of the essay so far. He begins it with the conversation he had with the reporter earlier that day, portraying the reporter in a negative light that he hopes is funny, because otherwise he thinks the reporter will reject it, punk-rock sensibilities be damned. He then begins to discuss the way white students speak when they talk to him and the way he hears them talk to each other. With him, they often drop words out of sentences as they imagine the rules of Ebonics dictate.

"Where you at last night?" they ask him.

"I was at home," he'll reply, emphasizing the verb.

"Weak," they'll say back. It's almost a modern-day parlor game, the way he and particular white students trade grammar when speaking with each other.

He moves on to discuss white flight in broad, simple terms, then switches gears and transcribes a rant he wants to get off his chest concerning R. Kelly, Kobe Bryant and Bill Cosby, and the expectations put on black males. As that begins to lose steam, he starts a new topic in the essay: the annual poetry slam and the black students' dominance of the art form. But he gets just two sentences into it before he feels writer's block creep in behind his eyes. He lays his notebook down beside his legs. He picks up the smaller, artier notebook for his poetry and starts to rewrite possible opening lines for his part in Da Trax's showcase poem. If he was thinking straight, he would realize the various opening lines, with their direct take on his personal politics, are thesis statements for his essay. Julius cannot cut himself out of his compressive emotional restraints when he works on the essay. Freed up by what he considers his natural medium, the opening lines strung together almost read like a poem in whole.

———◦———

John and Julius want Xavier out of Da Trax. X has a tendency to talk too much, and he has already offended the two of them with the constant vigilance of his nascent and uninformed black nationalism. He tells John to get rid of his "slave name." When he turns 18, X declares, he will change his last name to X to become Double X; a name, he says, with which no one can fuck.

Julius is free from such harassment because he is the anchor talent of the team and because not even Xavier would dare claim the name King unfit for a black man.

"That Black Panther shit got old in the '70s man," says Julius. "You don't see white boys running around with long hair and tie-dyed shirts talking about 'give peace a chance' anymore."

X just looks at Julius like it's the most ridiculous thing anyone has said. Of course the white boys still do that. They're always hacky-sacking at lunch, or crowding Amnesty International meetings after school.

"And if you do, you make fun of 'em," Jules responds to X's look. "Everyone makes fun of 'em. And for a reason."

"Well at least they're doing something, son," Xavier says, stepping to Julius as if to start a fight. "At least they got something to say."

Julius goes nose to nose with X, who is of the same height and stature.

"What?" Julius yells, as much a statement as it is a question. "What did you just say?"

"Your poems don't say shit, Jules," Xavier says. "You're scared to say anything, which is why you're scared of me."

Julius steps forward to take a swing at Xavier, but he is slow and predictable. X has already backed off, clearly more experienced in fighting. Julius's punch to the air feels like he is throwing a tissue. Before Xavier can come back, Damian and Malcolm grab him and carry him by the elbows out of their history classroom rehearsal space. Peter handles Julius easily.

"You're a phony, Jules," Xavier says as Damian and Malcolm push him into the hall. Julius says nothing as the door slams behind them. He waits for something to come to mind. After a brief moment, with nothing there, he turns around to walk back to his desk. John is miming a particularly lewd act, hips curving and pumping.

"Oh, Mrs. X," he says. "Why…uh…didn't you tell me you felt this way…ah…before!"

Peter crackles with laughter, but Julius turns away and reads over the poetry he has prepared.

———•••———

Three nights later, the night before the competition, Julius is awake with pains in his stomach. He sits stiff while Willie lies silent and straight in his bed, a single sheet pulled up to his throat.

Julius has the urge to wake Willie, the same urge that makes a vandal crash a brick through a window. He waits for it to pass and when it doesn't, he makes his way silently out to the living room. He ties on his Timberland boots loosely and grabs his black leather jacket before closing the door behind him and locking it, slowly inserting his key to knock down the pins one by one, like a magician demonstrating a trick.

He walks down Harvard Street, across the street from the apartment buildings, where a view of the sidewalk is blocked by the leafy elms that line the parkways. Julius kicks at rocks on the sidewalk, turns right, turns left, and winds up at Barrie Park. Like most open spaces in neighborhoods, the park is full of memories for Julius. He played T-ball here, launched an ill-advised foray into skateboarding, and witnessed a kid new to the neighborhood fall and hit his head on a rock, the muscles of his thin body twitching, contracting and bursting. Julius thought the kid was possessed, his spasmodic body moving as though controlled by ghosts with competing destinies.

The park is now inaccessible. A 10-foot chain-link fence surrounds it, a thick black curtain of scruffy material pulled tight over the inside like matted hair. Julius walks the perimeter of the fence on Harvard, where construction trailers and police tape and orange sawhorses signal that nothing is right.

He turns up Lombard, to the western edge of the park. John is supposed to be here, having agreed to a plan of subterfuge the day before. The two were to break into the construction site in a bit of suburban spelunking. Of course, John has not shown. The two have launched a hundred unfulfilled missions. Julius never even planned to show.

On Lombard, he can only walk up the west sidewalk, the fence extending all the way across the street and out to the curb. As he walks slowly, the abandoned houses to his left are dark, the residents all relocated. He thinks about when he was 10 and his mother was coping with the end of her relationship with Charlie, a male nurse from Des Plaines who would be her last boyfriend. He watched cartoons in the living room, the volume up high to stifle the sound of his mother crying. It was a queasy feeling, to be young and trying to hold onto the eccentric youthfulness of television cartoons, and to know that in the other room was a much more serious life unfolding. When he turned off the television and went into the kitchen, his mother choked on her sobs, as though she were swallowing bile. She wiped her face clean, and in an attempt to remove the signs of her crying, paralyzed the muscles of her face into a frightening smile, the kind clowns put on in nightmares.

Eventually, she gave up with a sigh and motioned for Julius to sit at the table. When he did, she remained silent, the tunes and gag noises of cartoons still detonating in his brain. After a minute passed, his mother stood up, put her hand on his head and said:

"You heard me crying, Julius?"

Julius nodded and she lifted her hand from his head.

"Well, that's nothing to worry about," and her slippers coarsely scuffed at the linoleum floor. "And someday we'll buy one of those houses over there so you won't have to hear any of that."

Now, looking at the homes with their shuttered windows and blank porches, all vitality swept off, Julius is glad his mother kept their apartment. He continues walking. The sound of the men working under the tent doesn't sound like men at all. There is a dull, low whir, like an old tree slowly cracking.

Near the end of the block, light cleaves through the Venetian blinds of a brown shingled house. The light is surprisingly yellow in contrast to the cold fluorescents lighting the work site. Julius heard there was one family who didn't leave, who stayed in their home with their windows taped shut and special filters on their central air. The reporter told him he heard the rumors, too, but any time he called or knocked on the door there was never an answer. He said one time he came by and there was music playing, Frank Sinatra, and when he knocked on the door, the lights went out and the music stopped mid-croon.

Julius lightly steps up the porch stairs, his weight not registering on the old wooden slats—he keeps his feet to the edges. He gets to the window and peers through the blinds, his vision a letterbox view of the family's life. Inside, a cat on a bookcase looks back at him. He scans the well-lit living room and sees no one, though there are signs of life: a remote control pushed between the couch cushions, a plate of crumbs, an umbrella left open on the tile. Julius thinks of the comfort inside this home, a stark contrast to the void of the black fence and the enervating low hum of workers carving out toxic dirt. He looks back over the park from his new, higher vantage point, the city stretching out behind it. The shabby bungalows and burned-out buildings, visible behind the park on the other side of Austin Boulevard, gnaw at a fear in Julius. He focuses instead on the white tent that crests in one corner of the park, and the enormous trucks, cranes and trailers that fill the rest. All around the perimeter, a frontier colony of air monitors spike trailers and fence posts. The reporter had said that if the monitors registered a rise in toxins, cancer-causing particles kicked up from the soil, the project would be shut down. The trouble with the plan: It takes two weeks to analyze the results. Anyone near the park could be breathing poison for fourteen days before they knew the difference.

Julius steps to the edge of the porch and fills his lungs with air, holding it in his chest and stomach until a deep sting invades his solar plexus. He does it again and again, exhaling slowly. He steps onto the sidewalk and turns right to walk home and thinks of Willie, sleeping in peace.

At the competition, students from all groups intermingle. Thugs and accelerated English students sit next to each other, college students home for spring break sit next to freshmen excited to be at an after-school event. It's one of the few times the lunchroom pattern Julius wrote about in last year's poem actually scrambles; black and white students don't sit apart from each other. The only segregation Julius can make out is that of student and family. Parents and younger siblings occupy the back rows, students the middle and front. In the very front are the performers and judges.

There is no big-name judge this year, just two Chicago poets Julius has seen before, when he and John made excursions to a couple of Wicker Park slams where they pretended to be 21. An Oak Park teacher is a third judge. The fourth is an English teacher from Chicago who is a poet—his every poem a dramatic reenactment of a conversation he's had with his Hispanic students. The fifth judge, the school principal, is busy meeting parents.

Julius can't find Willie among the crowd in back. His mother couldn't make it this year, pressed into more overtime at Loretto Hospital. Willie should be here; he and a few friends from Hawthorne were supposed to walk up here after school. He scans the back rows and then further down, further down, until his eyes land on the reporter.

Sitting in an aisle seat by himself, the reporter appears lonely. He has nothing on hand to read, no one to talk with, and as students buzz and flit and flirt around him in a dancing pattern, the reporter chews on the end of a pen. His eyes, behind thick-rimmed nerd-rocker glasses, seem open and empty, the way people make their eyes look when they die in movies. The reporter told Julius he would be there to write a story on the slam. When he said it, Julius thought he sounded enthusiastic. The face of the reporter now is not the face of enthusiasm.

"Calm down, man," Julius says and punches the reporter in the upper arm, knocking him out of his obsolescence.

"Man, as hot as this story is, it's Friday afternoon and I'm in high school again," says the reporter. "As soon as the results come in, I'm out."

Julius feels stung by the reporter's eagerness to leave. For the last two months, today is all he and John have talked about, and in some sense it led to his breakup with Ayana.

"No offense," the reporter says. "It's cool. It's just not the type of thing someone becomes a reporter for."

"Yeah, I hear that," Julius says, and continues up the aisle in search of Willie. He finds him among a group of admiring tweenage girls. The sight of his little brother makes Julius both proud and calm.

The contest proves less eventful than expected. X, who promised to get his own team together, instead staged a one-man boycott. A team of black sophomore girls gets the crowd on their side at one point, when one of the girls makes a reference to having sex with a teacher, but it's also the sort of juvenile shock tactic that immediately wipes them from the competition.

For their part, Da Trax fulfill the audience's expectations, blending just enough hip-hop braggadocio into their poetry to make it seem hip, but enough politics to make it seem urgent. At one point, Julius thinks they might lose when Malcolm slips in an unrehearsed line from a Talib Kweli song as if it were his own, a line about growing up past a time of "snotty tissues and potty issues." The judges seem oblivious, and when it's Julius's turn, the crowd is properly amped off John's introduction.

Julius opens with a dream analogy, touching on the Dr. King reference while being careful not to apply it to himself. He ends the analogy with him standing on Austin Boulevard.

Rock rock rock, I hear from the dude pushing crack, pushing pills
I don't need a doctor to tell me I'm ill

About 40 seniors explode into cheering. It's the type of line Julius puts into his poetry to approximate a rap lyric and get the crowd going. He feeds off the energy.

When one valve opens, the other closes in the heart
Shit on my mind but don't know where to start

The crowd goes silent as Julius lets a litany of his worries spin like a fishing reel. He drops the simple rhymes for a while and begins using just his meter to create a rhythm, and as he digs deeper into the poem, he makes oblique references to the air and cancer and environmental hazards, to love and friendship and revenge. The end of his 90 seconds comes to a close, and he feels as if the crowd has set upon him, surrounded him, absorbed him. He feels a neighborhood in the room. He looks up to the last row and standing on his toes in the aisle is Willie. He delivers his last line.

Have to watch what you lose when there's nothing to prove.

The judges smile and clap loudly but politely. The students do the same, only there is little of the whooping and calling that usually follow Julius's poems. Willie jumps up and down with pride. When the judges award Da Trax first place, the Chicago English teacher makes a brief speech about the sophistication of

"Mr. King's" poem, a speech to which no one in the audience listens. Julius doesn't even listen. He is simply glad it's over.

On Monday, and throughout the next week, Julius is surprised by the reaction of students to his poem. Everyone tells him they thought it was in some combination of: cool, deep, dope, freaky, ill, serious, scary, honest, weird, and powerful. Julius receives all of these adjectives both as compliments and as direct descriptions of his emotional state over the past few weeks.

When he sees Ayana out on Scoville Avenue after school, he approaches her with confidence.

"Hey Julius," she says, she being of an elite cadre of pretty girls allowed to call him by his full first name. "I saw you at the slam last week. Your poem was really interesting."

"Thanks," he says, and blushes. "It took me a long time to write it."

"I could tell," she says. "It was nice that you didn't call anyone a 'ho' for a change."

They both laugh, and instantly the nervous air of lovers comes between them.

She asks if he is going to participate in a Chicago slam for which he has been nominated. Julius is surprised she knows about it. He just found out yesterday. He says he will. She asks if he will perform that poem, and he humbly shrugs.

"City kids probably don't care much about that stuff," she says, matter-of-factly, as if it's something everyone has always known.

"I know," Julius says defensively. "That's sort of what the poem is about."

"I know," she says and starts to turn away. "I just think it's important for you to do it."

Julius looks at her, inquiring. Ayana returns his look, as if he is being coy. But Julius, at this point, doesn't even know what coy would look like. Over the past few weeks he has felt all cunning drain from him.

"You know what I mean," she says, and pauses with a smile. She rolls her eyes and Julius feels a sensation all over his body like melting and stripping away at the same time; like peppers over a flame. She breathes and says, "I'm just saying."

With that, Ayana turns and walks toward Lake Street, where a group of her friends are smirking at her for talking to Julius. Julius—for his part—is left alone and warm in front of the school wondering what, exactly, Ayana is just saying.

WROUGHT IRON

The kid likes my key ring. I can tell. Whenever I take a step or lean and it gives off that symphonic jingle, the kid smiles. It's something to consider. I unclip it.

I say, "You wanna hold onto this?" Stevie indicates yes with a slow nod, and I hand it to him like a soup kitchen volunteer. We're sharing some empathy.

"OK, OK," says the dad. "We don't need toys here, we need results."

Here is the situation: Stevie, a large-headed boy for seven, was dared by some now disappeared neighborhood urchin to stick his head through the family's wrought-iron fence. He did it, and one can tell he did it with no small amount of difficulty, given the scrapes along his temples, now seeping thin drops of blood. His ears are purple. His hair is stained to his forehead with sweat, the rest of it clumping and protruding from his scalp like feathers. His left eye is bloodshot, so much so that the pale gray iris is almost pink. Normally, he's probably a good-looking kid. But right now, he's pretty bad looking.

"Don't you have any tools with you at all?" The dad wants to know. This dad, get a load of him. Polo shirt tucked into his shorts. Cell phone in a holster on his belt. Something in his hair. I don't know what you call it. Gel? He called the fire department when he got home from work and found Stevie bent over in the fence, like a little hunchback, going on two hours. I came by this predicament a bit dishonestly, I admit it. Somehow, this dad mistook me for something I'm not. I'd been driving by on my way home from work—the dreaded 5am to 3pm shift cleaning offices—when I happened to see Stevie. I stopped out of curiosity, and the dad assumed I must have been some sort of rescue worker, my dark blue uniform with a fancy crest on the shoulder. He drafted my aid. I didn't correct him. I didn't have anything to do.

"No tools," I say. "We can probably make this work, though."

"OK, but we gotta do it before my wife comes home," he says. Yeah, I'm sure we do. According to him, we have exactly one hour before she returns.

I ask Stevie if he's tried bending over all the way, like he was trying to look through his own legs. He shakes his head. I tell him to tuck his chin and give it a shot.

"If he went in face first," I tell the dad, "maybe he can come out the same way."

We watch as Stevie folds himself, rising onto his toes, his back surfacing against the fence. Nothing happens for a moment. Then, the little guy grunts and we can hear the dull, tuning fork echo of the fence, or maybe it sounds like a whale. Stevie's head vibrates from the strain.

"Jesus, don't kill yourself, kid!" I say, and the dad snaps to and runs to his son, but unsure of where to put his hands, he just waves them around like Stevie is a crystal ball. Finally, he reaches through the fence and puts one palm on the small of the kid's back, as Stevie gives up and returns to his bent position. The scrapes by his eyes are now weeping blood.

"God, Stevie! Aw god!" the dad says, and he runs inside to boomerang back with a handful of paper towels, pressing them against Stevie's temples like he's blotting his makeup. We both encourage the kid that, should we again suggest anything that makes his face tear open, he should just stop. He nods slowly. He hasn't said a word since I've shown.

"Is he always this quiet?" I ask the dad.

"Lately," he says. His cell phone rings. From the tone of the guy's voice—one of panic—I'm guessing it's the wife. Stevie watches his dad with worried eyes.

"You don't like to talk, huh?" He trains those eyes on me. I can't decide which one I should look at, the clear one or the bloodshot. "That's fine. But how about the next time we do something that hurts that badly, you just pop the whistle on my key ring in your mouth, OK? Give it a toot, and we'll stop."

Stevie gives me a look like he doesn't like the idea of more painful options. Tough luck, kid. Shouldn't have put your head through a fence.

"That was my wife," the dad says. "She's actually 30 minutes away." Beneath his tone it's all written large for me and Stevie. Dad's been screwing up lately. Mom is sick of Dad screwing up lately. Mom's not going to like finding her kid held hostage at the neck, as though trapped in medieval stocks. There's so much fighting, Dad can't tell anymore when he is responsible and when he's not to blame. Anything is just another rock on the pile.

I ask, "What have you got for tools?"

"A hammer," he says. "And a screwdriver." He pauses. "And some screws."

We pace. I convince the dad to pull on one post while I tug at the other, and Stevie pulls his head through as best he can. This sort of fight, man versus metal, doesn't really get you anywhere, but even the slightest perceived give makes you feel like a juggernaut. The dad can feel it, he looks at me and smiles like we're two tough guys. But that's all dashed when Stevie puffs on the whistle, and he's back to hanging his head through the fence posts, his ears pinched and near blue. The dad suggests butter; buttering the kid's whole head, slicking it down like a piece of meat and greasing it through the posts. Stevie, though, does not like the idea, and is blowing the whistle before the dad can even reach the front door.

The dad and I take a stroll toward the house to discuss our

options out of Stevie's earshot. We're both low on ideas.

"Are you married?" I don't know why the dad asks. I'm not wearing a ring. "I don't mean to bring you into all of this, but we gotta get Stevie out of there before my wife comes home. I don't want to fight in front of him again."

I nod. I wonder if this man is in the life he deserves. Does he have a good heart in this mediocre shell?

The dad thinks we could ice the fence to make it expand, but then he admits he doesn't know what he's talking about. I send him inside the house to look for anything that could help. The two of us pacing behind Stevie, out of ear- and eyeshot, is making the kid nervous.

I pick up a slim but sturdy branch near the sidewalk. I jimmy it between Stevie's head and the right fence post, create some space, and try to leverage him through. The whistle blows. I pull on his waist, the whistle blows. I grab his forehead but the kid knows what I'm thinking and the whistle blows.

"I don't have any kids, Stevie," I tell him as we wait for the dad. "But if I did, I'd bet they'd do stupid shit like this on a regular basis." Stevie's eyes go wide at my curse, but then we both share a chuckle. It's the first noise the kid has made from his own voice box, and it reminds me of how long it's been since I've heard a kid laugh. I ask him why he doesn't feel like talking, and he shrugs. "I get it," I tell him.

The dad walks out with a sleeve of Ritz Crackers in his hand. Stevie looks ready to devour, like the excitement alone could turn his other eye bloodshot. We have about 15 minutes before the wife comes home, and it's only now that I've started thinking about her. She works later than her husband. The two of them are probably a happy couple who have, recently, begun to fear that their happiness is paper-thin. She and her husband fight more than they once did. He makes her feel like the bad guy. She's probably not so bad.

"Let's really think," I command the dad. And we stare, frantically, at Stevie.

"I'm going to concentrate," the dad says, as if telling me this will somehow free his son from the fence. He chews a cracker with purpose.

His cell phone rings and he answers, turning his back on us. Stevie puts his eyes on the ground, and I move quickly. I grip the kid's head like a basketball and give it one giant shove, the weight of my massive belly giving it enough torque that the kid's head makes it through halfway, but it's not enough to break the line. He blows the whistle so hard that it falls out of his mouth and clatters to the ground. The tips of his ears are white.

Stevie shouts, "Aw fuck!" and the sound of his voice makes both the dad, who has quickly hung up the phone, and me laugh. Stevie, who can't see us because his head is now frozen between two bars, staring at the crumbled pavement of the sidewalk, isn't laughing.

"I'm sorry, Stevie," I say, sucking back the laughter. "It's just that, well, when you get older, you'll understand. Hearing little kids curse is the funniest thing." The dad nods and laughs. The dad reaches over and feeds a cracker to Stevie who lets the crumbs jump out of his lips like popcorn. He wriggles his head and it pops through again.

"We need to do something soon," the dad says.

The threat stings us both, somehow. The dad looks at me. His kid's in pain and he doesn't know what to do. I take him by the shoulders, and we hatch the final plan.

The dad walks behind Stevie and raises his feet, turning him parallel to the ground. I then turn Stevie, who slides his arms through the fence, as though he were Superman flying in an alley.

We're methodical. Surgeons. There is meaning in this work, and the dad and I can both sense it. We're gathering purpose. The dad pushes a few inches, I pull a few more. Stevie is wincing now, without his whistle, but he's braving it. His shirt is up, and I can see that the metal is chafing his skin, little curls of white dead cells flake off. This kid is good. I imagine that in the future, we three will have a statue raised to us on this spot, and we'll be posed just like this. We'll be heroes of some forgotten tragedy.

A gray car turns into the driveway and out steps a woman in a black suit. She's frightened by what she sees: a stranger and her doofus husband playing tug-of-war with her big-headed son who, it should be noted, is still spotted with blood about his face.

She wants to know what is going on here. The dad fills her in, our momentum frozen with his kid hip-deep in fence. The dad tells her the story, points to me when he gets to the part about calling the fire department. I nod professionally. She asks Stevie if he's OK, and brave little Stevie nods. As she goes inside, she declares all she has to do is change and then she'll be right back to help, straining to stay polite in front of me. There's a tension here that makes me believe in my role as rescuer. I'm disarming a bomb. As soon as the door shuts behind her, the dad says, "We need to make this happen now."

Our movement of Stevie through the fence, I imagine, is of the same sort of labor that jewel thieves employ. Quiet, deliberate and desperate. There's a moment when we hook his hips that makes me think this whole thing was a bad idea, but the dad is now so anxious that he pushes through, and Stevie gives no indication this hurts him more than anything else. We're now taking this work to another level.

When Stevie pops free, I don't fall backwards. It's not like uncorking a bottle. There was resistance, and then there wasn't, and then there's Stevie, his little forearms like dowels in my calloused hands, stumbling to stand with me holding him like that. I let him go and he smiles, twists his neck like an athlete, and offers his hand up for a high-five.

The dad is more ecstatic than anyone, "Yeah, Stevie, yeah! That wasn't so bad, right?" He's licking his thumbs and smearing the blood on Stevie's face. "We did it." He looks at me, and as his wife jogs out the door in shorts and a T-shirt, looking not bad I have to say, he says, "We fucking did it."

The mother hugs Stevie, but stands a moment later to discuss this with the dad. The mother and the dad, the husband and the wife, sink quickly into an argument. Stevie's smile is erased, and so is my feeling of accomplishment. The mother and the dad are screwing this up. They aren't trying to think. They're not looking for new ways to get unstuck.

I bend down and pick up my keys, shake them once for Stevie's pleasure. I crouch and give him another high-five. I look over his shoulder at the mom and the dad and say to him, "Don't worry, Stevie, they're just scared. It'll be fine."

"Thanks," Stevie whispers back to me, "But how do you know?"

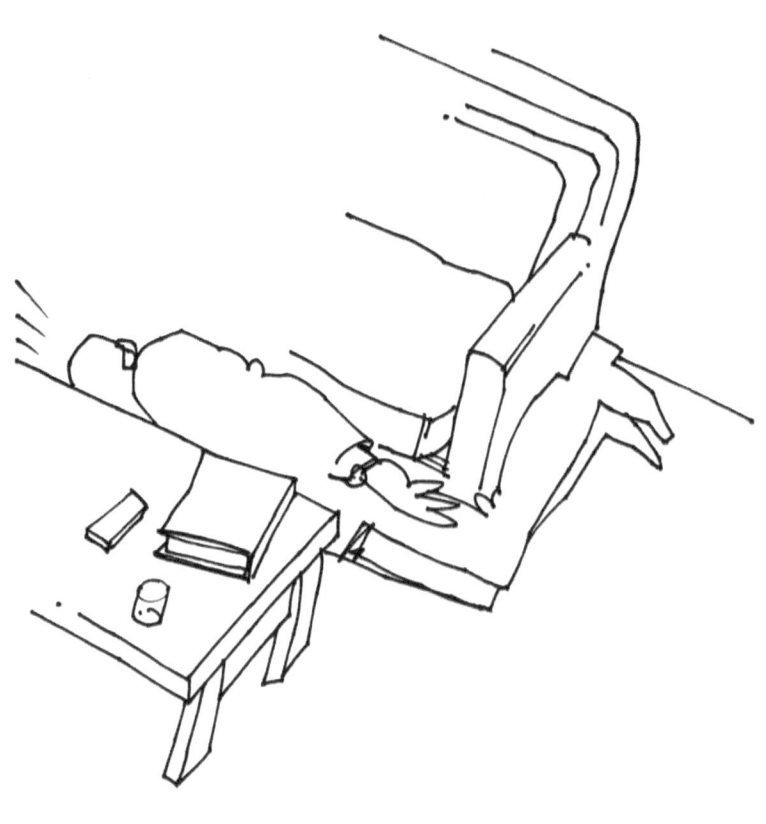

WE WILL ALL WRITE A POEM

As you're reading this story I want you to imagine that, about 15 feet in front of you and a little to your right there is a large machine that looks like a giant ear of corn. This contraption is approximately man-size if we, you and I together, can agree that I am approximately man-size. The leaves of the husk are made of what looks like stainless steel and the cornsilk is made from fine, sparkling, translucent crystal that, at certain points in this story, will kindle orange. But not yet. I'll tell you when that happens. Also, at certain points in this story, someone will enter this contraption and upon entering will proceed to operate it through various levers and buttons and gizmos that will become apparent to you. And when that person engages these various devices you should make the sound that the machine would make. It would go something like *hummina hummina hummina*. I would be grateful if we could practice this very quickly, and there is no better way to read than to participate, so please say it aloud: *hummina hummina hummina*. Also, on the right side of the corn-shaped machine large red letters spell out: **HUMMINGBIRD**. And on the left, it reads: **THE**.

Over here to your left and closer to you like, say, your heart, we have a void. It's nothing. Imagine that. Imagine it however you can. If you have to picture this area as entirely gray or entirely white or entirely black, go ahead. Feel free to close your eyes when we shift to this part of the story. If you can imagine nothing, literally see nothing, that would be great, but also I would like for you to e-mail me once you've finished with the story.

In this void is a boy of 15. Still prepubescent. Perhaps the only boy of 15 without pubic hair who could be happy about such an arrangement. Or, he's not happy, but neither is he upset about it, which his parents and older brother are. His doctor is not upset, but curious. This is not why the boy is in this void, or at least he would tell you there are other reasons.

Polishing the leaves of The Hummingbird, the old man who built her still can't remember exactly how it happened. He woke up at four in the morning Monday the week before, poured himself a cup of coffee and sat on his back porch. He was by himself. All of the colors in his backyard were faded and there was no such thing as sound. To break the silence the old man said the first thing that came into his mind: "Loneliness is a type of violence." And then he rose, entered his garage, and began work on The Hummingbird.

The boy in the void got this way on a dare. Or at least, he dared himself. He came home from school one day and decided he was going to write a poem about how much he hated the kids at school, but that would have been like every poem in the high school literary magazine, *The Third Rail*. He decided to write a poem savaging every poem in *The Third Rail*, but then he stopped before he started, because tearing apart clichés was cliché. So he did nothing. He just sat on the edge of his bed and did nothing and thought that maybe that was the strongest rebellion of all. He thought: I should do nothing, and go nowhere. He became nervous at the thought. His feet tingled and the small of his back tensed. He said to himself, "I fucking dare you to go nowhere." And here he is. In the void.

The Hummingbird's wings are tensile, like the tail of a cat or a kind of leather, but plated with metal banged out of the bottom of kitchen pots. The husk of The Hummingbird is truly a work of art, the kind of work that you create in a fever over the course of a few hours or days or, if you're lucky like this old man, a week or so. It's a matter of how long you can sustain the self-delusion that there's no reason to doubt your work. For most of us, this is a matter of minutes. For this old man, it has traditionally been less. This is the first time he has staved off the self-doubt for such a long period of time. It is like he learned to walk, and then entered a marathon.

The boy cannot dare himself to leave nowhere. He has found his gift and that is to imagine nothing. He sees neither color or light nor the absence of either. He is upended by his own imagination, and he is unaware of both his body and his lack of awareness of his body. He is not hairless, his voice neither unnaturally high nor disused, his parents neither concerned nor pretending not to be concerned. He doesn't think about writing poetry. If he wanted to not think about his daily trappings he couldn't, because nothing requires that he not even think in negatives. It is a perfect state.

Hummingbirds are the only species of bird that can deliberately fly backwards. Plenty can be blown back by stiff winds or have difficulty because of injured wings, but only hummingbirds have a reverse gear. Think of that for a moment. Imagine if, as humans, we could all walk only forward except for, say, Ohioans, who could walk backward. What would that mean? It would mean that we non-Ohioans would always be trying to have sex with Ohioans. Because we'd want our kids to grow up better than we did, namely be able to walk backward on occasion, even though, maybe you can't even remember the last time you walked backward. But it would seem like such a luxury.

The boy doesn't think of the girl. He can't think of the girl when in the void, but, it should be said, the girl is not what you think. She is his best friend with whom—despite a very academic lesson on kissing technique conducted during the watching of a boring movie—there has never been a mutual attraction. To be clear, neither has ever tried anything on the other, because neither has ever wanted to. Before he dared himself into the void he thought about that a lot and wondered whether that desire would ever show itself.

We don't know how long hummingbirds have been around. For a long time, scientists thought maybe only a million years or so, which isn't old for a bird. In 2004, Dr. Gerald Mayr of the Senkenberg Natural History Museum in Germany identified the remains of two 30-million-year old hummingbirds, a long past extinct species found in Germany, where hummingbirds typically don't live. The extinct species was dubbed *Eurotrochilus inexpectatus*. Translated into English, that means *unexpected European hummingbird*. These little guys were so alone that the fact that no one knew they existed was written into their name. That is why this old man called his contraption "The Hummingbird."

The boy has discovered a game. It's a game he's played for a few months on excursions to the mall with his mother. He wanders department stores beside her and sees it in the eyes of her fellow shoppers as they throw him sidelong glances, as if squaring their shoulders to him would be an admission of guilt. And he notes the employees' hesitation at how to address him alongside his mother. He ignores them as they say to her, "What is your son looking for?" or "What did your daughter have in mind?" He doesn't correct them if they get it wrong, doesn't lie to them if they get it right. He wants the confusion inside him to be felt by someone else. He loves it like nothing else. He'd like to talk with someone about the game, but so far he has said nothing.

The old man is now inside the machine. He pulls the lever again. He presses three buttons and the crystal above his head kindles an orange that is almost red. Imagine a tropical flower and then light it on fire and you have the color. The Hummingbird could be a rocket. It could be a generator. It could be a flying machine or its opposite, a drill. It could be some sort of 15th-century-imagined, 21st-century-realized youth machine that would keep the old man alive for centuries. You and I cannot tell. The thing is: The old man has no idea what The Hummingbird is. He is nervous inside. It is cramped. He is more aware of his frame's small size now that he is inside this slightly larger than man-size contraption. The tensile leaves of The Hummingbird fold down. The old man is afraid. He doesn't know what he has built and he's sure anyone from the outside would think it a time machine but he's not sure if it is or, if it is, how he feels about that and you're supposed to be saying *hummina hummina hummina* right now but you're not so fuck it.

The boy is slipping out of the void. He has thought about the game, about his conflicted feelings toward his enjoyment of it. That conflict, by necessity, is both positive and negative. He thinks of something now and is coming out of it, out of nothing. He finds himself standing in his room, near his desk. He says aloud, "Nothing sucks." He thinks this may make a good line in a poem to send somewhere. He, now in his room, in the world and in his body, reaches for the small pocket notebook that he carries everywhere but on which he has never written a thing.

The old man does not know what pressing the final three buttons will do. He presses one and the tensile leaves of The Hummingbird unfold into wings. He presses another and the crystal's orange reddens. He has one last button to press and has become convinced now, as I'm sure we all have, that this is a time machine. Yet the old man is one of those who is lucky enough to be no longer curious about his past.

The boy is no longer in the void at all. He is in his room, which could look like a desert were cacti and animal skulls traded for cheap boys' room furniture. The boy sits at his desk to write the poem. It does not occur to him that by leaving the void he has begun a disintegration, a making of nowhere into somewhere. But that is not important. What is important is that he has written a poem. It contains one line: Saying "nothing sucks" is just like saying "everything sucks." The title of it makes him smile. It is called, "When I finally write my first poem it will be called 'Fuck You.'"

Building The Hummingbird, the man thinks, is a way for him

to tell the world that he knows this is as far as his future goes. He presses the third and final button and a small microphone rises out of the front and the thrum of The Hummingbird's wings tells him he is about to go. The Hummingbird will fly forward or backward. Feeling none of that violence of loneliness, he slowly leans into the microphone as if to smell a flower, parts his lips in the quickest of breaths and whispers, "Nowhere."

THE BIRDS BELOW

The first time I got caught in Graveyard Alley it was scary as hell. We peered around the last in a row of trees overlooking the above-ground pool of the house behind them. It was sort of a tradition, as we struggled to become more deviant, to lift a clump of brick from a pile at the end of the alley and hurl it into the pool.

The pool was always deserted, as if there to tease kids stranded too far from the beach in the hot New England summer. This time, however, a hairy man bobbed in the water. He looked shorter than either of our dads, but with the pool walls it was difficult to tell.

Brad and I had just come back from the baseball card shop, a daily ritual we practiced for a year, before I entered the eighth grade and Brad the sixth. The Hairy Man looked like Pete Incaviglia, the chubby slugger whose rookie card Brad prized from a grab bag that day.

The Hairy Man dipped into the water and up came a woman. She looked about the age of the Hairy Man, but all women over 21 looked the same to me. She wasn't wearing a top, and the fullness of her breasts shocked me. I was 13 that summer and had seen a few naked women in movies by that point, models in soft-core flicks Cinemax showed late at night. A few of us would sit at sleepovers and cheer when the woman took off her shirt, and then we'd sit in silence and wonder at what happened for the rest of the scene.

This woman, however, did not have the glow of movie light on her breasts. Her breasts were reddened from the sun or touch or both, and they fell away from each other with a freeness I'd never witnessed in my late-night education. Her face looked like a lunch lady's.

Brad looked at me and whispered that we should take off. I was frozen. Something seemed wrong about their openness.

"It's not right," I said.

Brad, squinting to see, hissed something but it was too late. The brick was already flung, the arc already peaking like a story with an obvious ending. Brad was paralyzed, squinting because he refused to wear his glasses and the sun was brutal off the surface of the chemical pool water.

There was no splash, only a thud, and I dragged Brad back through the alley.

A word about the alley: it's not at all an alley in an urban sense. It was two ordered, parallel rows of pine trees, with about 9 feet between them. The ground below was always covered with stale, rusty pine needles, a function of no sunlight and little foot traffic. My brother Harris and I were the only ones who used the alley until I showed it to Brad. Its main function was to cut off the Ausoff's house, which fronted the busy Dodge Street, from the Hairy Man's house, whose address was on the quieter Gary Avenue.

Harris and I laid claim to the alley, even though it wasn't on our property. It was an easy way to get directly from our backyard to Nelson Avenue, the center of the neighborhood's social scene, without having to travel the circuitous path of side streets. It was an old privacy border, the kind you find all over New England, but Harris and I eventually turned it into a sort of car pool lane for kids. We named it Graveyard Alley when I was in third grade and Harris in sixth, because that summer bird carcasses started turning up in the alley. There was no rash of bird deaths on the news, no new dog in the neighborhood. They just kept showing up. Some were putrid and oozing like fermented peaches. Some were stiff and salt-dried like jerky.

It went from being an inside joke between Harris and I, to a shared mystery, to an unspoken observance. We kept the name Graveyard Alley, but stopped mentioning the birds. Confronted with that much death, even the joke seemed worn thin.

It was across this ground that I dragged Brad. His feet were coming alive, staggering to keep up. After the brick hit, there was a stark pause—followed by a grunt, and then silence. The grunt came again, built into a growl and then two screams that were so loud they were almost childish. Their cries were quickly muted, and as Brad and I pushed out through the side of the alley into the Ausoffs' yard, we slowed to listen. Brad, whom our baseball coach forced to wear glasses because he kept getting hit by fly balls in left field, swore the brick hit the woman.

"What if it hit her boob?" he said.

"Gross," I whispered.

We quieted as we heard the Hairy Man scuffle up the embankment that led to the alley.

Secreting around the corner of the house, Brad gasped as he saw the bowl-bellied man emerge into the alley: his body hair matted and his prick still half erect, hanging and twitching spasmodically, as if searching for ground water. I tried to pull Brad away but he was mesmerized. It was the first time he was confronted with a naked grown man.

"He looks like a friggin' apeman," Brad said.

The Lunch Lady moaned from the pool, and the Hairy Man turned back, abruptly cursing the trees. A dark gutter ran from his right shoulder through his back hair. It was blood, and it ran all the way down to his butt, which looked like two candlepin bowling balls stuffed in grocery bags.

"There's blood on his ass," I said. "It definitely hit the guy."

The Hairy Man yelled something, and Brad and I scrambled to our own homes.

I was hesitant to tell Harris at first. I was so confused that day in the alley and unsure what I did was right. The answer seemed obvious enough: it's never right to hit someone with a brick. That seemed like natural older brother advice.

Harris, however, was a strange older brother. He was a natural athlete with a broad build that prevented him from ever gaining a true athlete's quickness. He was actually downright slow, and his athleticism came from his strength and grace. He dominated in pickup basketball games because he was so tough underneath, and he was famous for breaking the Conants' window behind Brown Field with a home run. He went to the front door, retrieved the ball, and did it again 10 minutes later. He apologized again and raked their leaves every Thursday for a month. He taught himself to hit lefty.

But despite all of his natural ability and the confidence it gave him, his slowness made him always seem like he carried a burden. He didn't seem slow, he seemed slowed down. I think because of this, his temper was something of family legend.

"Yeah, maybe you went overboard," Harris said, two weeks later when I got up the nerve. "But hey, the old perv was probably asking for it. I mean, what if old Mrs. Ausoff had seen them? She'd probably drop a crutch."

Harris poured his third glass of lemonade in a row and guzzled it down. He was just back from lacrosse practice. He cut me a deal: if I came and got him the next time it happened, he would give me his Fred McGriff rookie card. I was sure it would never happen again.

"People who get hit by lightning keep playing golf," he said. I had no idea what he meant.

That Saturday night, Harris asked our mother if he could borrow the car to take a girl to dinner. Mom agreed so long as he took me along.

"It'll be good for Matt to get out of the house for once," she said.

Since the Hairy Man incident Brad and I had pretty much kept indoors, playing Nintendo and pricing baseball cards. We never talked about it. Because Brad was younger, he wasn't one of my friends who watched Cinemax. I didn't think I was old enough to think about that lady, never mind Brad.

"Ma, I was out last night at practice," I said. I knew Harris wouldn't mind if I came along, but I also knew he'd appreciate it if I tried to get out of it for him.

"Take Brad with you," she said. "If he can't go, you can stay home."

I called Brad and of course he agreed. Neither of us had anything to do and we were going to Woodman's, a famed indoor/outdoor seafood restaurant in Essex that had the best fried clams in a seafood region. As we waited in the car outside Brad's house, I turned down the car radio.

"Hey Harris, sorry Mom made you take me and Brad along," I said.

"Forget about it," he said, looking out the window.

"I just know it sucks."

"Don't fucking swear."

Harris punched me twice in the arm and shoved my head into the window, which made a hollow thud.

"Jesus, you got a brain in there?" he asked.

"Not anymore," I said, wincing.

Harris laughed and rubbed my head. Brad came out and got in the backseat of our mother's old Zephyr station wagon.

"You couldn't get the Honda for a date?" Brad asked, thinking he could get on Harris's good side by razzing him.

"The key is to get the date, Boy Wonder," Harris said as he pulled out onto Enon Street. Harris always called me Batman and Brad Boy Wonder when we were together, the implication being that Batman and Robin were gay.

Courtney Bresnahan, Harris's date for the night, was the kind of girl only high school boys seem to find attractive. She had a bone-thin, curveless body and her hair was cut in a fancy European way, obviously cribbed from a magazine. It sliced down along her chin line and was longer in front than in back. I described it as "retarded" to Brad. Her skin was pot-roast brown thanks to spending the early summer jobless and at the beach. She wore a bikini under her tank top. Harris told me earlier they had kissed at Crane's Beach last week and were "going out" ever since.

"She made out with you before you even went out? Isn't that skanky?" I said, still learning the ropes of adolescent affairs.

"You got a lot to learn, Batman," he said, without elaborating.

At dinner, Harris and Courtney sat on the other side of the room from us, per her request. Brad looked petrified.

"I've been going back to the alley lately," he said, tossing his clam strips with his fork.

"Yeah, what for?" I tried not to show any interest.

"I don't know. I can't get it out of my head. It was so weird I want to see it again," Brad was talking quickly now. "I've never seen anything like it, and I thought it'd be cool to catch 'em again."

"You're a perv," I said, biting into a crab cake.

"No, I mean, I don't need to see it," he said, embarrassed. "I'm just curious. Do you think they were doing it?"

"What? Cut the shit," I said. "And stop going back there without me. You're just going to get us in trouble."

"Yeah, well, I don't think I can go back anyway."

Brad had been running through the alley when he'd heard a man call out from the pool. He never looked back.

We sat for the next ten minutes in silence, looking across the restaurant as Courtney and Harris made out.

"Dude, do you think they'll do it?" Brad asked.

I didn't know the answer. I picked up my tray without saying anything and threw it—tray and all—into the trash.

I thought I could avoid Courtney the whole night, since she'd asked Harris to sit apart from us and didn't say anything to me beyond "hi" when she got in the car. But Harris stopped for ice cream and she waited in the station wagon to stay warm. Brad and I went with Harris, but when my brother found out I didn't want any—my stomach throbbed—he told me to get back in the car and keep Courtney company.

"Just don't go cheating on me," he said.

Courtney and I didn't speak at all and it seemed the line for ice cream was like those lines for bread we'd seen in a school movie about Russia.

"So," she said, sighing. "What's it like being Harris's little brother? Intimidating? You know, he's so much bigger and older than you. That would scare the hell out of me if I were you."

I didn't know what to say. Harris had his temper, but mostly it kept me in line. Nearly every time he'd flown off the handle at me, I was asking for it.

"Well, he's bigger and older than you, right?" I asked. "But you're going out with him."

Courtney laughed.

"Jesus, do you guys always stick up for each other?" she asked.

I didn't know what to say so I didn't say anything. I slipped down, flat on the back seat of the wagon, kicking the driver's seat to let off a little steam.

"I didn't mean anything by it, Matty," she said. "I'm just messing with you. You and your brother just seem so different, 'cuz you're so scrawny. But I think it's cool you guys are cool with each other."

"It is," I grunted.

"My brother and I never talk," she said. "He's a total douchebag."

I laughed out loud, not expecting a girl to talk like that.

"That's awesome," I said.

Courtney was pleased to amuse me. She flipped down the visor and wiped her lipstick off in a napkin.

"Can't have black raspberry ice cream with cherry lipstick, know what I mean?"

So far, Courtney hadn't called me Batman or shoved me or threatened to "make my life hell" when I got to high school like my brother's friends.

"How long are you going to go out with Harris?" I asked.

She laughed again and spun around to sit on her heels, grabbing the headrest with both hands.

"I don't know, how long are you going to be his brother?"

"Forever," I said, without thinking about the strangeness of the question.

"Then I'll stick around for a while, too," she said, looking down at me. "He's pretty good to us, huh?"

I didn't say anything. She gave me a high-five to seal the agreement. I figured out why high-school guys like girls like Courtney. I didn't even notice that outside, a high-school kid had cut in front of my brother in line and Harris now had him in a full nelson and was pushing his face into a fence post.

In the next couple weeks, as summer reached its peak, Courtney was around a lot. That summer was particularly hot. We had one baseball game canceled because they were afraid the kids might get heat stroke.

Our mother didn't take to Courtney at first, the way all mothers mistrust high-school girls who carry themselves with her vigor. But Mom warmed, as everyone did, to Courtney's honesty and fearlessness. She was one of the prettiest girls in school but chose field hockey over cheerleading.

Sometimes, when Harris was busy or out, Courtney would come by and hang out with me. She'd let me show her my video games and baseball cards, but mostly we just watched bad talk shows together. One afternoon we watched a "Ho'Down" competition on Richard Bey. Two women in giant boxing gloves, sports bras and mouth guards squared off against each other over a guy.

"This getting you hot, Squirt?" She called me names like Squirt and Shorty but it never bothered me. She always rolled her eyes when she said it, like she was making fun of the people who used those names, not me.

"I don't know, they're kinda skeezy, don't you think?" I said. "And why are they fighting over that dude. He's only got like four teeth in his whole mouth."

Courtney laughed.

"People always protect what they got," she said. "If some girl tried to steal Harris from me, shit yeah I'd fight her."

I punched her twice in the arm for saying "shit."

"You do not punch me, Shorty? Got that?" Courtney rolled over to me. "You do not punch me."

She pinned me to the ground and grabbed at my ribs and under my chin. I was laughing and helpless and crying. I kicked and kicked but that field hockey made her strong.

She yelled and fake karate-chopped my thighs, making me laugh even harder. I thought I was going to choke. I started to get nervous that she might feel the erection forming in my shorts. If my mother didn't come downstairs to break it up—and to shut off the Richard Bey—I might have tried to kiss Courtney.

It was my first betrayal of Harris.

In August, I dragged Brad to Bayberry Beach. Apparently recovered from the incident, he wanted to sit inside and play video games to stay out of the heat. I should have been hanging out with guys my own age, but my closest friends decided they wanted to play football and spent much of their time lifting weights and hanging out with other Pop Warner players. Mom told me I shouldn't lift at 13—it could mess up my bones—so I went to the beach to watch women in bikinis.

When she was there, Courtney would let me sit near her friends. They were older than me and noticed me only when I brought them hot dogs or Italian ices from the snack bar. I tried all sorts of ways to get their attention. When Brad and I played paddleball my movements were short and jerky as I kept my biceps flexed the entire time. I positioned games of Frisbee so I could make diving catches in front of them, bouncing up like it was nothing, though I knocked the wind out of my lungs more often than not.

A few short sprigs of hair poked through my underarms that summer, and I checked on them every morning before showering. When I lay down on a blanket next to the sunbathing high-school girls, I'd lie on my back and with one hand play with my underarm hairs—all five of them—to show them off. I even started to use Harris's Right Guard deodorant because it would come off in small clumps, accenting the hair.

One night after the beach, I walked across the street to Brad's. We were going to watch the movie *Major League* and make frappes in his blender. When I got there, his parents already had their coats on.

"Hi Matty," his mother said and squeezed my shoulder as she walked across the kitchen to get her purse. "Brad's dad and I have a function tonight, so we'll be out."

Brad's dad was a dean at Boston University and his parents always attended "functions," vague adult parties that seemed both glamorous and boring. I was about to ask what it was when his mother stopped in front of me.

"You know Jessica, right? She's going to babysit Brad tonight," she said and slid out the door with her husband. "Have fun!"

Over on the couch, Jessica stood up and turned around. She was in my grade, and we'd been in school together since preschool. Jessica and I were friendly enough; the way boys and girls are sort of friendly in middle school. She smiled.

"Hey Matty, I didn't know you and Brad were friends," she said, slipping a glance to Brad. "That's so cool."

The way she talked made me wince. I knew she thought it was definitely uncool. She said "cool" the way kids did when someone showed off their initials on their backpack, or talked about a vacation to New Hampshire. She said "cool" the way you do when someone your age is best friends with your babysitting charge.

"So I hear you two want to watch a little movie and make some frappes?" she said. She was trying to be nice, but it wasn't helping. The one friend I consistently hung out with that summer, and Jessica was mature and old enough to get paid to watch him. And, in turn, she was watching me.

"Actually," I said. "I just came by to say 'What's up.' I'm hanging out with my brother and some of his friends tonight."

"What?" said Brad. He jumped off of the couch and frowned.

"Yeah, sorry man. I forgot." I slid my arm back in my coat sleeve.

Brad looked like he might cry.

"Well, OK," said Jessica. "Don't sweat it Brad, you and I are going to hang out tonight. Are you sure you don't want to make a frappe before you go, Matty? It'll be so fun."

I thanked her, said no, and walked out. I didn't care if Brad cried. It was just further proof he was too young to be my friend.

I came home and went straight to our bedroom, before Mom could ask me what I was doing. I opened the door and Harris was lying on his bed, phone pressed to his ear.

"Oh yeah?" he said. "That sounds awesome."

He was speaking in low tones. I'd never heard him like that before.

"Uh, Courtney?" he said, flustered. "Can I call you back? Batman's back from Robin's, and he looks pissed."

He hung up the phone and I flung myself down on my bed. I picked up a Green Lantern comic from the floor between us and pretended not to notice his stare.

"Dude," he said. "What the fuck?"

"What?"

"I thought you were going over Brad's tonight. It's 7 o'clock," he said.

I decided to hold nothing back. Hanging out with Brad and a babysitter who was my age was humiliating, and I knew Jessica couldn't help herself: She would tell everyone. Harris listened as I raved.

"I'm sick as shit of being young," I said. He didn't punch me for swearing.

"No one cares about shit like that *unless* they're young," he said. "So if you stop caring about it, people won't treat you like you're little anymore."

It seemed reasonable; except I didn't know what else I was supposed to care about.

"What you need is to get a girlfriend," he said. "Girlfriends make you forget about all that other shit."

"Yeah?"

"Hell yeah," Harris said. He jumped on the throw rug and splayed his arms. The rug slid beneath him and he acted like he was surfing across the room. His T-shirt molded to his shoulder muscles. "Girls are tough, but they're worth it."

He stopped just before the door.

"You're all right, Squirt," he said. "You're a funny kid, but you'll nab one."

Over the next couple weeks, school got closer and I started thinking about what girls I would nab in eighth grade. Baseball was over, and Brad and I didn't see each other at all. I still used the alley, somewhat curious what I might find there; but there was never any action, never anything worth seeing.

I didn't see Harris much, either. He and Courtney seemed to cool off and he spent most of his time in double sessions for football. He was nervous about losing his linebacker position because of his lack of speed, and the incident at the ice cream shop meant he would be suspended for the first game. I mostly avoided him, knowing his temper would be quick. I woke up one morning to a crash in the kitchen. Harris was making a shake before practice and our old blender was chopping and mixing erratically. Out of patience, he pitched it to the floor, shattering the glass. When I got to the kitchen, the tile was splattered with a green-gray mixture that sparkled with glass and clumped with bits of banana. Harris was out the door.

One day, after a game of touch football, I came home and

Courtney was there, watching talk shows in the basement. I hadn't seen her in a week, but as always she was in her summer uniform: a tank top and short shorts, a bikini beneath her clothes. She sat on the couch and dangled a giant flip-flop off her big toe. The cool room smelled like the rosy scent of a teenage girl's sweat.

"Hey Shorty," she said as I came downstairs. "Where you been?"

"Where's Harris?" I asked, opening the trash barrel that held a bunch of our sports stuff and slamming the basketball down on top of a lacrosse glove.

"Practice," she said. "You down on Nelson?"

"Yeah."

"Harris was telling me about this thing you and he use to go back and forth," she said, not taking her eyes off the television. "What's it called? Graveyard Station or something?"

"Alley," I said. I opened the mini-refrigerator and pulled out a Capri Sun. Harris won the fridge in a school raffle. "Graveyard Alley. But it's just a place between some trees."

"I wanna see it," she said. "Come on, I've cooled off enough down here. I need to get out in the sun while there still is some."

Courtney and I walked out into the driveway. I opened the gate to the backyard and as we walked across, she nearly tripped over the Frisbee Harris and I used for home plate when we played home run derby.

"It's like a minefield out here," she joked.

It was true. Aside from the home plate there was a softball, all chewed up from when I was mowing the lawn and accidentally ran over it. The mower shot it out and it missed Harris's leg by a few lucky inches, denting the bulkhead to the cellar. He punched me twice, but it didn't hurt because neither of us could stop laughing.

We got to the alley and I ran in front of Courtney and bowed at the entrance, the way I had seen a conductor act when my class visited the Boston Symphony. Courtney laughed and I followed the line of her giggle down the muscles of her neck to the place where the U of her tank top stopped. She bowed back slightly, and the crest of her breasts peeked in from both shoulder straps before disappearing behind an orange bikini top.

"Too kind, sir. Too kind," she said as she passed by. I followed her in and was immediately overcome by the mustiness of the alley. A rain the day before had wet the old needles on the ground and the pine trees still held the moisture. It gave the alley a muted heat I hadn't noticed when I'd passed through before.

"Wow, it's so cool in here," Courtney said, halting a third of the way in. The Hairy Man's house was still visible and I checked back for any action. "I mean, it's like another world in here, you know?"

She sat down, not caring if she got her shorts wet, and crossed her legs. I turned to keep from staring at the spot where the leg of her shorts fell open.

"Sit down," she said. "It's not that wet."

I sat a few feet away, keeping my eyes on the Hairy Man's house.

"Tell me again why you guys call this place Graveyard Alley," she said. "What an ugly name for such a great place."

"A bunch of birds died here a couple years ago," I said. "It was pretty gross. We don't know what caused it. They just started turning up."

Courtney hummed in agreement. We sat still for minutes.

"Why are you staring at that guy's house?" she said. I heard her skid over the distance between us and she leaned into me to follow my gaze. The apricot smell of her sunblock mixed with the soily smells of the alley. I swallowed hard.

"Oh, Brad and I saw these two old people fooling around in the pool about a month or so ago," I said, trying to keep my voice straight. "They got all pissed. So I'm just looking out for them."

"Fooling around, huh?" Courtney said, leaning back off me and sliding her legs next to mine. "You ever fool around with any girls, Shorty?"

I didn't say anything. I crossed my legs to hide my arousal and pretended to look deeper at the Hairy Man's house. I looked into the sliding doors and through the blinds. I could barely make out the shape of furniture. I wondered if the two—the ape-shaped Hairy Man and the Lunch Lady with the sunburst breasts—were in there now, doing as they pleased.

"Huh?" Courtney said as she teased my neck with her finger, trying to tickle me just below my ear, where my jaw line turned. She knew it always made me laugh. I didn't laugh this time.

I grabbed Courtney's wrist and carried her hand away from my face and shifted my weight onto my left hip to turn. I was too rough, I felt her wrist flinch in my hand and I let go quickly, sending me off-balance and toppling into her. My face mashed against her breast, but all I felt was the padding of her swimsuit. Her smells exploded in my head.

"Whoa, Shorty. You drunk?" She still had no idea what I was doing.

I raised my head and gave her the look I saw on all of the male stars of those Cinemax movies. It was the look I thought I saw on the Hairy Man's face that day when the Lunch Lady first appeared above the surface of the water, breasts bared to him. I saw it on Harris's face, just before he kissed Courtney at Woodman's.

"Oh no," she said.

I parted my lips slightly–Harris said to do that–and when I felt her lips near mine I slipped my tongue out. It collided with her lips immediately, but it felt like hours passed before my lips followed suit. I swirled my tongue around, painting the front of teeth and sliding along the underside of her lips. I had no idea this wasn't how it was supposed to work.

"Uhhnnnn," she said. "Ewwww."

I took her sounds as moans of pleasure. I grabbed the back of her head and slid my fingers through her hair. They got caught in the sandy and salty gnarls the beach gave her thin hair, and I tried to work my hand through. I just pushed our faces closer together and found it hard to breathe, my nostrils stuck to her cheek like a slug under a rock.

I pressed on, balancing my hips to free my other hand. I tugged at the bottom of her tank top.

Her fist caught me sharply in the gut, the claddagh ring my brother bought for her tearing my shirt slightly and scraping a thin swath along my ribs. I exhaled and fell to the right, rolling down and hitting a log on the ground, the old wood responded stiffly to my stomach. She kicked off her oversized flip-flop and gave me a heel to the kidney. I whimpered slightly. She breathed loudly.

"You're my boyfriend's brother, Matty," she said. She hit me hard in the back of the head with the sole of her shoe, slamming my nose into the log. "But that doesn't mean you're not fucked-up."

She kicked off her other shoe and picked them both up to run off. I rolled over and the stones beneath me slowly bruised my back. She was gone. Blood seeped down my cheek, a warm stripe on my face. I lay there, looking up into the treetops of the alley, listening to the evening birds sing. I didn't cry; I knew there would be plenty of time for that when Harris showed up.

But he didn't come. I lay there until the shade outside the alley was the same inside, and everything looked brown and orange. I sat up and waited longer.

The Hairy Man emerged from his house, sliding open his patio doors. Again, he was shirtless, but this time wearing teal shorts with tiny fluorescent sharks biting at each other. Dry, he was far less imposing. He hadn't shaved in a few days, drawing lines around his jowls and smudging his moustache. His sleepy hair was tufted in the back like a cardinal's. I watched as he picked up a net and ran it skimming along the water to corral leaves and needles. His grace was astonishing, and I was shocked that this man didn't do everything in the same monstrous manner he'd chased Brad and me through the alley.

The pain in my back forced a cough out of my lungs and the Hairy Man lifted his head from his work. He peered into the alley.

I sat silent, and the darkness of the pines hid me well. He stalked a bit closer before he was out of the patio light and gave up. He passed around the pool until his back was to me. Though it was dark, I could see under his deck light that there was no mark from where I hit him with the clump of brick. He didn't favor either side and there was no interruption in his back hair. He paid me no mind. He whistled while he cleaned, and it became just another noise mixed with the crickets, mixed with the birds.

I lay down on the needles and waited for Harris to come get me.

YOU CAN NEVER FORGET

This is a motivated memory.

You are standing, 16 and scrawny, in the hallway of your girlfriend's house. Sun hot from the window at the far end of the hall. Your shorts, which are really your girlfriend's father's shorts, pillow around you as you grasp at the waist and cinch them to your hips. You are half their size and they feel heavy even to hold. You wear nothing else and you think of your boxers tangled in her parents' sheets as her grandmother stares at you, face dusky from the sun behind her.

"This is just unbelievable," she says and is unashamed to look you in the eye. "And disgusting!"

You beg her not to call your parents as your girlfriend scrambles for her clothes in her room. You realize, by the grandmother's snarl, that as far as she knows, you broke up with your girlfriend last week.

You tell her that if she calls your parents, it will be worse than she thinks because your relationship with them has been rocky of late.

"I can see why!" she says, voice booming behind clenched teeth.

She isn't letting you walk away to get your clothes. You thought you were sweating when you were in bed. That was nothing.

This is a motivated memory. This is a memory that is forcing its way back from the bottom of your vault and crawling over birthday parties, Christmas parties, make-out sessions and success stories. It is pushing aside live-and-learn memories like the time you bumped that Volvo in the beach parking lot and took off, or when you fell asleep in a class of four, or when you got caught lying about your financial stability.

This memory has a purpose and it will stay buried no longer. It will rise to the top and plant its flag and wave until you take notice and stop glaring at your son's girlfriend, 17 and hipless and straight, a hand towel and two arms covering what she can.

She's frozen, waiting for you to say something. Your son is in the shower. His music is loud.

But until the memory gets there, you need to stay calm. You feel it spelunking through tunnels and winding up paths. You need to avoid saying anything stupid.

"Get your goddamn clothes," you say.

That was perhaps a bit too forceful but at least the poor girl doesn't have to stand there anymore. So far, so good.

Another memory jumps up for a flash; it's the time you were caught drinking on the eighth-grade ski trip. This memory is always there, though, brought to the forefront because you're still friends with those people and you tell this story often. When Mr. Druin caught you, all he did was take the beer and call you a hooligan. It is circumstantial, funny, juvenile and innocuous. You shrug. It teaches you nothing.

It is a lazy, unmotivated memory.

You reach for the doorknob to the bathroom as the ambitious memory, a missionary among the savages, builds its church at the base of your tongue. It all comes back to you; how you heard the grandmother call up the stairs and how your girlfriend silently screeched, pushed you out of her and ran down the hall. You searched for your boxers but there was nothing and all you were left with were the dusty dad shorts under the bed.

You remember the mortification. How going from teenage sex to nearly butt-naked in front of grandma was like diving from a rock quarry and skimming too close to the cliff. How you never thought an old woman could hate so quickly.

This memory has a lot to say.

You remember walking out of the house, the grandmother screaming for you to shape up, and how you had to walk the eight miles home. There was a late summer chill in the air and you, while now in your own clothes, were still only wearing a T-shirt, shorts and sandals. You contemplated not going home, sure that your parents knew and were waiting.

You remember how hungry you were, but felt sure you would vomit anything you ate.

But then there's another side to this memory, and you remember how good it felt to be with your girlfriend again; that if the two of you could get through this, maybe you would grow closer. In fact, aside from the beer memory (which at this point has sunk back down) your life up to that point had been without any sort of bad streak, any greasy skidmark.

The memory's church bells are ringing.

You remember how young and burning you felt. You were independent and under your own rules that brought you together in evermore dangerous ways. Grandma caught you and you walked out with your head up. You and your girlfriend were finally naughty. You were badass.

The memory's choir is singing.

You knock on your son's door, open it a crack. She sits alone on his bed, shivering in full clothes. He's still showering. You turn back.

"It's OK. I'll drive you home now."

On the way home, you tell your son's girlfriend that she's not in any sort of trouble. Things like this happen and are no big deal. You ask that maybe she could tell your son to turn down the music when he's in the shower next time.

　　She says there won't be a next time.

　　The memory packs up shop.

WINGED ATTACK

The American-born kung fu master does not have his father's respect. The son is brawnier, tattooed up his arms and on his legs and handsome in a way that makes his female students dislike him. His forms class is unrelenting, the stance work keeping the students' legs bent at the rigid angles of furniture. Signs of weakness are met with cutting punches, tearing muscles in almost religious fashion.

Still, the American-born kung fu master does not have the authority of his father, the grandmaster. On this day, the grandmaster interrupts his son's self-defense class and makes him kneel. He says, "The best way to practice kung fu is with a smile." He laughs. The students all laugh. But they know that it is better to suffer the son's punches than the father's aphorisms.

Grandmaster calls up a young male student and instructs him to assume a fighting stance, which the student does with technical vigor and rigidity. "See?" says grandmaster, his smile a crescent moon. "Is this how you're really going to fight? If someone comes up to you on the street and wants to take your wallet you're going to say 'Haw!' and get into stance? No. You're going to put your hands up and try to back away right?" And he laughs. Everyone laughs. Everyone is nervous.

"Look at me. I'm perfectly relaxed," says grandmaster, grinning. The young male student standing in a fighting stance begins to relax and smile. He chuckles along with grandmaster. Nods his head. But grandmaster is now at the student's throat, his fingers straight out and depressing just below the student's voice box and entering his neck about two inches, and then his hand is back to his side without anyone seeing what happened. He was here, smiling, then there in the neck, and now here, smiling. It's like cheap animation. The student coughs and tastes blood. "See?" says the grandmaster, "It is much easier than you think." He motions for his son to stand up, and just like that, the American-born kung fu master is disgraced.

The following midday, the American-born kung fu master cooks grilled cheese sandwiches and chicken soup for his wife, five-year-old son and four-year-old daughter. They have just moved into a new bungalow on 95th and Kimball, far away from the north-side school and grandmaster's home.

"Mmmmm," says his wife. "I love the way cooked cheese smells. It reminds me of being sick as a kid." She moves in tight behind him and grips his stomach, a hold he has no defenses for.

He stirs the pot of soup and flips a sandwich. The phone rings and neither of them answer. It feels good to answer to no one. After lunch the American-born kung fu master lies on his floor in his U. of I. sweatpants and blank T-shirt and plays a video game with his son.

"Boom!" yells his son as his gunman on the television screen lines up and takes down the kung-fu master's. The kung-fu master rolls onto his back and grips his chest as if dying. His son leaps and yells "Boom!" again, dropping an elbow to his dad's stomach. The kung-fu master's reflexes bring a knee into his son's shoulder and this makes his son cry for eight minutes. This happens often. It is difficult to be a father and a kung-fu master.

The American-born kung fu master ices his son's shoulder and when he is done, the son remains on the couch to watch college football. The father returns to the kitchen table to sit with his wife and daughter, who is counting the pennies she has collected in a plastic Donald Duck bank. The wife and husband sort through utility and medical bills.

"Have you thought, hun, of going back to work?"

The American-born kung fu master and his wife have had this conversation many times. The school is not making money. Quitting his day job has become a great strain on the family budget. The kung-fu master puts his face in his hands and pulls on the skin of his cheeks until his eyes become colorful teardrops.

"We'll see," he says.

Three generations of kung fu men walk together down the aisle of the North Riverside Toys "R" Us. They are searching for a toy bird feeder, for the youngest. The youngest is fascinated by birds.

Needless to say, the grandmaster does not approve of this at all. He shows it by walking four steps ahead of his son and grandson. Toys "R" Us being Toys "R" Us, it is nearly impossible to find anything and every aisle seems to either have a video game or a Barbie doll in it. The three call over a clerk to help them locate the feeder. The grandmaster steps in front as the clerk approaches and smiles big like a dental exam.

"My son cannot find this bird thing for his son. Maybe you can show him around?"

The clerk, maybe 40 or 42, has no idea that he is in the middle of the most explosive internal kung fu fight he will ever witness. "What sort of bird thing are you talkin' bout here?" asks the clerk.

"A feeder," intercedes the American-born kung fu master. "My son is a young scientist."

"Sure, you're talkin' toy feeder," asks the clerk.

"Yes," says the grandmaster. "Maybe it is in the girls' section?"

The clerk waves them forward. The bird feeder is in the girls' section. The three generations of kung fu men must walk through an aisle of pink and another of purple before they find it. The American-born kung fu master feels no shame at this walk, only anger toward his father. The youngest should not have to be disgraced simply for an interest in nature. That is not in line with how they have been raised.

The next day, the American-born kung fu master rises early and descends to his backyard in the dark. He practices, pounding his feet into the dirt where there once was grass, flowing crane style into drunken monkey into way-of-the-fist-in-the-little-forest, all of which forces what leaves are left on the trees to sway and drop like tiny suicides.

In class that day, the American-born kung fu master makes his students nervous. He punches a lazy student in the chest and it sounds, upon leaving the student's body, as if he has been stabbed. During a self-defense drill, the American-born kung fu master calls up the same student from the week before. The student is displeased. The two assume a fighting stance again and the American-born kung fu master begins his lesson by asking the student to punch him.

The grandmaster arrives and interrupts again. He laughs and throws back his longish hair.

"What? Is my son teaching you this stiffness again?" he asks, smiling. "Relax," he says, "This is not the military. I am not Forrest Gump. This is kung fu, it's an art form, it's—" He delivers a knee to the side of the unhappy student's head, who drops to the floor.

"See?" he asks the class. Everyone nods.

The American-born kung fu master does not kneel, as is custom when his father takes over. The grandmaster, unsure of what this means, tries to act as if it is part of the show. He signals to the shaking student that he may sit down, and the kid crawls slowly back into line. Neither the American-born kung fu master nor the grandmaster notices.

"So," the grandmaster says. "You all have seen me strike you students and you probably think it's easy. Oh sure, I've been studying for 50 years and have defeated champions in both hemispheres and may have even stopped my opponent's heart in one match. But you are new to the arts. What would it be like if

I fought my son, right? He is stronger, he is younger and he has trained for more than 20 years. Of course it would be a–" The grandmaster lashes out with a cobra strike to his son's throat. His son, who has been entranced by the smell of cigarette smoke on his father's breath, is caught off guard. He tastes his blood.

"It would be no different than fighting any of you."

And then he is at his son's throat again, but the son is not there. He has stepped forward and to the side. His father, momentarily stunned, does not feel his son's winged attack, two palm strikes to the grandmaster's cheekbones, another two fists to his solar plexus. The grandmaster does not taste blood, but rather, instantly, begins sobbing. The class sits and watches, as the grandmaster cries, unstilled, for a full three minutes until he asks: "Where did you learn such a hideous style?" sounding like a man underwater. "I cannot stop weeping."

"It emerged from your cauldron of shame," says the American-born kung fu master. And the students watch as the grandmaster weeps. And weeps. And weeps. There is no end to this crying.

After class has been dismissed, the American-born kung fu master puts his father in the passenger seat of his car and drives him home. They pass through the soulless sheen of Lincoln Park and the humid stupidity of Wrigleyville. The grandmaster is still weeping, unable to control himself. The old man is curled into his seat, wiping at his face, struggling against something. Something in him has been undone by his son's strikes. They make their way into Uptown, where the grandmaster has lived since his wife left him. The car rolls slowly past the old buildings, the American-born kung fu master stretching the time in the car with his father. There is an unidentifiable pleasure to watching the grandmaster weaken, a feeling of happy regret, a deeper understanding of mastery. But, the son begins to worry that the uninterrupted weeping may actually be unending. Like much of his long relationship with his father, he cannot tell if he was in the right. So much control has erased any sense of limits.

The American-born kung fu master pulls into a metered parking spot and locks the doors behind him. He returns a few minutes later, finding the old man's tears in a slow, unsteady stream. The steering wheel's grips are wet, but there's no other sign the old man has moved. The American-born kung fu master hands his father a six-inch Subway turkey sandwich, extra mayonnaise, light on the pickles. The two men eat their identical sandwiches, wiping their mouths with their napkins. The young master and his father eat in unison, alternating bites of sandwich and sugar cookie, thinking the pleasures in life, at the very least, are simple.

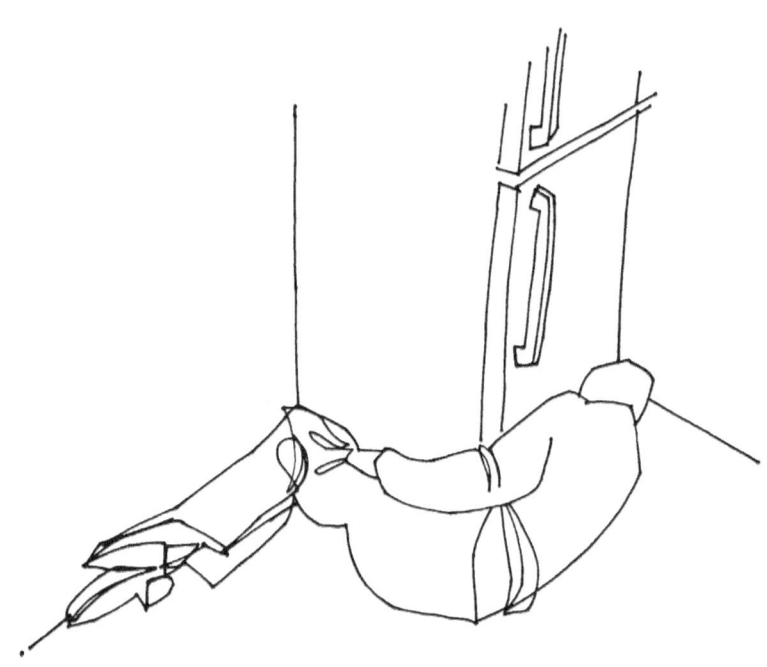

CHRISTMAS SPIRIT

The angel walks around my apartment like an appraiser. Its gait is unsteady but confident, its eyes alert even though—according to it—it has seen it all. It shows me its wings now and again, the tips peaking out of a thin white smock.

The angel doesn't bother to hide its disdain for me.

"See you soon," it says, then picks up my VCR and carries it out the front door. I can't stop it.

This is how it began:

My son Joey came over for Christmas. And when he said he was going to get me a Christmas gift this year I thought, *This is going to be the cutest.* It was meticulously wrapped by his seven-year-old fingers, which means that it was in an unexpected shape still unknown to mathematicians. And it was enclosed in reams of tape, as if whatever was inside had to be suffocated before given to me.

When he got to my last gift to him, he stopped, let out a sigh, flopped onto his butt and looked at me as though drunk and stupid with happiness. He said, "All right Dad, open mine."

We argued for a moment about whether he should just finish first but he won when he said, "Why are we arguing on Christmas?" I lifted the item off the mantle, shook it, made ridiculous guesses at what it could have been. An elephant. A palace. My very own football field. He didn't think the jokes were very funny.

I finally started in, ripping and biting at the tape, digging my keys into all of the layers of scotch and masking. Joey joined in, impatient with my sweating and heaving. I held it and he hung from it until a piece of tape let go. And finally, after much work and the last resort of scissors, the thing just sort of opened. And there in my hand was a refrigerator magnet. A clay phone with wings on it. A rotary phone to be exact, which I don't think Joey had ever seen before, being seven years old and oblivious to history, not to mention communication technologies. Inside the rotary was a little pink heart.

"Don't you like it?" he asked as if I'd just hurt him.

"Are you kidding me?" I said. "What's not to like? Now I can put stuff on my refrigerator all the time."

He seemed happy and opened his last gift, but I have to admit that I didn't really pay attention to what it was.

"Joey," I said later, the two of us watching a claymation Christmas movie, our bellies full of eggnog ice cream. "What do you think your gift to me is?"

"A magnet."

"But a magnet of what?"

"A phone. God, are you stupid?"

"But what kind of phone?" I asked.

"It's an angel phone."

And that was sufficiently cute to get me to stop asking questions, which I think he does on purpose.

When someone gives you a gift you don't understand, it's as if they've handed you a riddle they expect you to already know how to solve. It's a trick to test how connected you are. But I couldn't crack Joey's code.

The heart on the angel phone glows red sometimes. It ignites into a crimson that almost looks like the heart is bleeding. The first time I noticed, I was putting a six-pack of Hamm's into the crisper and when I shut the refrigerator door, the kitchen lit up red like a movie version of hell. I thought it maybe had a battery, or was one of those glow-stickers that absorb light during the day. I flipped on the kitchen light, and the thing stayed the exact same brilliance. It was freaking me out.

I touched it, and it ran as cold as the refrigerator. The wings stayed the same dirty, lazy clay construction but that heart, it glowed like it meant it. The first night it ignited, I fell asleep on my kitchen floor watching the angel phone shine red like a siren. When I awoke, there was the angel, making a big show of impressing me. The red glimmer of the heart was replaced by the angel's sweet vanilla incandescence. It didn't speak as it floated around the kitchen and into the living room and back. It had tangerine-colored hair all the way down to its charcoal skin. Its gender was nonspecific. Its body was not curveless, but neither did its curves give it away. It gave me the same feeling I'd get when I wandered into a clothing store and couldn't tell which stuff was for men and which for women—a panicky dread that I'd always look the fool.

"You," it said in an androgynous voice, the way the elderly of both genders sound when they've smoked all their lives. "You need to get your shit together."

And then it picked up my stereo and floated out my front door.

Joey came over the next day, dropped off by his grandmother, my ex-girlfriend's mother. It's difficult to see her, they look so alike.

"Hey buddy," I said. "I want to talk to you about this gift you gave me."

"Yeah, what about it?"

"Well, first of all, I love it. Man, I love it."

He looked at me like he couldn't understand why I would lie.

"I do, really. It's just that—I was thinking—do you really think it's an angel phone? 'Cuz, here's what I was thinking: Maybe it's not. Maybe it's a dead phone, that's flying up to heaven."

"How did it die?" he asked.

"Short circuit," I said. "Old and frayed wires."

He looked at me like I was senile.

"Could have been disease. Violence. Or, sometimes, things die because we don't love them enough."

"Does that happen to phones?"

I said "maybe," because that was easiest.

I explained to him about the heart. About how sometimes, late at night, the heart brightens the whole room with an eerie blood red and scares the shit out of daddy.

"And what do you do?" he asked.

"Well, normally I fall asleep on the floor because I can't stop looking at it."

Joey hung his head. All his father could do in the face of the magical was lay down and go to sleep. To be truthful, his father felt the same way about himself.

"I know it glows red, dad," he said. "That means you're

supposed to answer the phone."

"And do you know about the angel that comes out?"

"Let's watch a movie," he said.

When I'm alone at night, the heart flares, my eyes itch and go bloodshot and I fall asleep. I wake up and there is the angel. It doesn't bother floating anymore or phosphorescing. It looks haggard, like maybe it sleeps on its floor, too.

Always, it has vague advice. One time, I awoke with the kitchen rug under my head as a pillow, and it said, "Even if you collect two crumbs of food and some aching feet, you will still be hungry." Another time, it said, "Treat women with the same respect you reserve for the military."

Most often, I wake up and the angel paces in my kitchen or slams through the drawers in my bedroom. There were plenty of occasions when I thought, perhaps, the angel wasn't an angel at all. So when it slouched into Joey's bedroom one night, I got onto my feet and for the first time, I followed it. It threw all of the blankets off my son's bed and pulled any toys stashed below it out into the room.

"Why do you buy your son these horrible toys?" it asked as it pulled out an inflatable boat and a broken toy microphone. "You should take him with you to the store next time. Let him pick it out."

It was the most specific the angel's advice had ever been, which made me feel like I'd somehow failed to solve Joey's riddle. It reached deep under Joey's bed and pulled out an old Nike shoebox, tattered on the edges like a small animal had been cutting its teeth on it. Creases ruined the sides and top. It looked old and tired.

The angel turned toward me and lifted the lid. Inside were Joey's baby shoes, a scrap of clothing, a few Polaroids, some drawings and a few things like shells and rocks he'd collected when he was younger. There wasn't anything inside Joey's memory box from after he turned five, a full two-year absence. It was as if he'd stopped living. The angel left the box open on the floor and walked through me into the kitchen, tossing an invisible rope around my neck. As the rope tightened, it extended its hand like an evangelist and the microwave tore from its wall brackets and floated to the angel's palm. It jumped out the window, and though I didn't move, I stopped breathing and listened for a crash that never came.

Before the last time I saw the angel, I fell asleep and dreamt. I lived in a giant loft space, the kind you see in '90s movies where the new rich live—all brick walls and refinished hardwood floors, like trees were created to lay beneath for your bare feet. My ex-girlfriend, Joey's mother, was there, the first time I'd seen her in three years, if seeing her in a dream counts. I sat in a chair and she next to me. I had my shirt off and she had started in on a tattoo on my upper left arm. She said she was out of tools, so she just carved an outline of what she wanted there with an Exactoknife—a homemade prison tattoo. It didn't hurt. She leaned in close and I thought, *This is what true angels look like.* She had the same stark, starless sky hair as in life, and her lips were red enough to make a dress out of, and I thought *what the hell*, so I kissed her. And we kissed for such a long time that part of me knew it had to be a dream. My mind could stretch it out as long as it wanted. We kissed until it seemed we were ready to keep going. I unbuckled my belt, but she backed away, looked at me and said, "Hold on.

I'll be right back. Don't go anywhere." She worked the long walk out of my apartment as though the whole dream was a lead-up to her runway debut, closing the door behind her. She never came back. And for some reason, my mind stretched that out, too. I sat for hours, waiting and hungry for the kisses of a girl who left me alone in an apartment that wasn't even mine. I don't need anyone to tell me how pathetic it is to dream of being stood up, and then to sit and wait in that dream for something that you know is never going to happen.

When I woke up, if this is even possible, the angel was crying.

"You have no idea what you're doing," it said. "You have no idea how to teach your kid anything, because you'll never even try something." It stumbled over to me like it was drunk.

"That doesn't even make sense," I said.

"Oh, so you're arguing with angels now? You sleep on your kitchen floor at night and you're arguing with angels?"

"I don't even know if you are an angel."

He whirled around the apartment, crazed and I think desperate. There was nothing left for him to take. Everything of value was gone. That morning, I had brought all of my remaining valuables out to the back alley and left them there to be scavenged. Anything tied to a memory or meaning was donated to the Salvation Army. The only thing left in the kitchen was the refrigerator, and if the angel took that, and the magnet along with it, it could never come back.

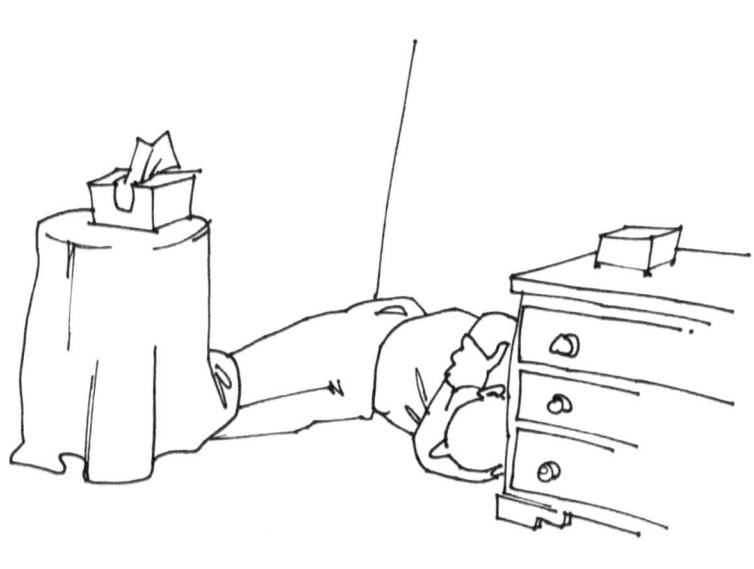

BIG DOUG RIDES TORCH

I've been thinking of getting a moped. My neighbor Doug has a motorcycle, a hulking Harley Davidson VRSCD Night Rod. The thing is a plasticky blue, a color mostly associated with miniature-golf water traps. He works on it every Sunday in his driveway, literally spit-shining the chrome. We argue about it sometimes at neighborhood barbecues.

"That thing guzzles more gas than you do beer, Doug," I say.

"Who cares? It's a thing of beauty."

"It's a thing of eco-terrorism."

"You ever dance with metal in the pale moonlight, Johnny?"

Given enough beers or social pressure, Doug will refer to his McHenry County Motorbike Enthusiasts' Club as a gang. His motorcycle gang. It's a little game I play at barbecues. I find children are the most active catalysts. Afraid to look like a weekend canoodler in front of the kids, he'll do his best to impress them.

"When we get on the highway, we ride four strong," Doug says. He's not joking. He delivers this speech like a military commander. "The right and left wings we call Thrust and Parry, respectively. The one up front, we call Torch. The one in back, Cashmere."

Doug's wife Claire watches all of it from the shade of the big ugly tree in their backyard.

"No one with a moped was ever called Torch," Doug says, pointing at me.

The first time Claire and I had sex, she was nervous afterward, her feet bouncing under the sheets like knitting needles. Doug was away at a Harley trade show for the weekend; we couldn't be caught. But that was guilt talking, not fear. Now, when we're through, she lays her head on my stomach, and I drape an arm across her chest, in the smooth slate just below her neck. This particular time, Doug is out on a ride with his club. They've gone to the mountains, where they'll fish and, failing to catch anything, eat the frozen hamburgers they've brought along.

"Maybe I should leave him," Claire says.

"And run to me?"

"No," she says. "Probably not."

We fall asleep.

I haven't looked it up yet, but I'm pretty sure that if I had a moped, I could outrun a cheetah. I remember cheetahs being able to run up to 40 miles per hour in short bursts. I could get a moped up to 35 mph, which means that so long as the cheetah was sufficiently behind me, if I had a head start, I would be completely safe. I don't know when this became the standard for my mode of transportation, but it has. I need to be able to outrun something, some vague danger. I start checking newspaper ads.

When Doug gets back from his trip, something is different about him. He's out in front of his house all the time now with his Harley. Every day he tinkers. He wears a toolbelt while he works, and the thing seems light on his hips, his belly eclipsing the pliers and wrenches that hang from the front. I watch all of this from the second-story window of my house. I make my way down to my driveway and look across at Doug and his house. Our houses look the same, the paint variations on the same light blue, the asphalt of my driveway slightly grayer, having been most recently tarred two years before Doug's. His house has flower boxes and flower beds. That's what separates them. Nothing grows on my property.

It's been hot and wet all week, but tonight is the worst of it. I'm on my third T-shirt of the night. I walk over to Doug, who gives me a nod as he fiddles with something under the fuselage of his Night Rod. Fuselage may not be the right term. So I ask him:

"Something wrong with the fuselage?"

"Would you even begin to understand what I'm doing down here?" he asks, without looking back. "Inside here is a Revolution V-Twin power plant."

I have to admit, it sounds impressive. I notice he isn't sweating.

"That sounds like a lot of power, Doug. You need all that?"

"That depends," he says. "Just how deeply you delve into the night, Johnny, is up to you."

I nod and walk back to my house. From upstairs, I watch him pace around the motorcycle and dive in at different spots, the way I'd imagine a painter might finish up a masterpiece, though I've never seen a real artist work. Across the way, a window lights on the second floor of his house. It's Claire. She stares out from the glass with hollow eyes. I flick the light switch twice. On, off. She begins to undress.

There's a guy on Craigslist selling an Italian moped for $325, just in my price range. We make arrangements over e-mail for him to come over and show me the ride. When he arrives, I realize it's a she, not a he. She pedals up into my driveway. It's morning, and when Erica—I see now that I just ignored that last vowel in her name—sits down in my kitchen, the light through the window is on full, like someone has lit us for filming. We drink iced tea and talk mopeds. There are things that I know and things that I don't. Moped is short for Motorized Pedal Bike. Knew that. All around the world, moped riders meet up in local branches of the Moped Army. Didn't know that.

"Is that like a gang?" I ask Erica. She looks at me like a patient surgeon.

"It's an army," she says. "Wanna go have a look?"

Back outside, Erica and I inspect her moped. It's shiny red, with what looks like new tires and new pedals. She says she has to sell it because she's moving, otherwise she wouldn't dream of giving up on such a beautiful piece of machinery.

"Why do you want a moped?" she asks.

"I don't know," I say. "I just like the idea of something being both man- and machine-powered."

She nods.

"Well, this will get you 100 miles to the gallon," she says. "And you can get up to 30 miles an hour."

"Oh," I say. That clocks ten miles slower than a cheetah. "Well, is there a way to make these things go faster?"

"Sure," she says, her voice bubbling. "It's called derestricting.

You can look it up on the Internet."

"Done." I write her a check and roll the moped behind my house, out of Doug's sight.

———•—•———

Claire wants to know who the girl was. Doug is out on one of his nighttime, lone-wolf rides, where he gets out on the road just to clear his mind. I tell her that I just bought Erica's moped, nothing more.

"I can smell her on you," Claire says.

"That's impossible."

"I don't mean literally. Besides, it's not like I'd care."

We're lying in our normal position, but on the floor. I get up and walk over to the computer. I type "cheetah" into Wikipedia. According to the website, the cheetah can get up to 60 miles an hour in short bursts. No derestricting in the world would double the speed of my new bike. In the wan light of the laptop, I must look pathetic, because Claire asks what's wrong.

"I don't think my moped could outrun a cheetah."

"Hun," Claire says. "There are more important things you need to outrun, and a moped isn't going to help you with any of those."

Later, she falls asleep in my arms, feeling heavy.

———•—•———

"I see you bought yourself a motorbike off a little girl," says Doug. "Good work. Maybe now you'll buy that surround sound system you've always wanted from a deaf guy."

"I'm sleeping with your wife," I say.

"Yeah, I'm sure you are," says Doug, laughing. "How'd that happen? She liked your Little Miss Ridealong?"

I look up at Doug's house and Claire is nowhere to be seen, but the entire scene, the house, the flowers, the crispness of their lives together, is so lovely. You could move a movie set in here tomorrow, and it would be a blockbuster the next day. It feels untouchable.

"Mopeds get 100 miles to the gallon," I tell Doug.

"Good for them," he says. "But do they purr like this?" He cranks the handle of his Harley and the sound is so loud it feels inside my head. When it stops, I feel empty.

———•◆•———

My first ride on the moped is a disaster. I motor/pedal down to the Whole Foods, but there's no real storage for my two bags of groceries. I hook them onto the handlebars, but their weight is too great, as is their inertia. Just as I'm turning onto my block, the one on the right rips and spills my vitamins, hummus and frozen pizza onto the ground. The sudden loss of weight causes the moped to list left, and the other bag slides off. I don't have the dignity to stop and clean up my mess. I just accelerate, the buzz of the motor sounding like an old electric knife, off in the distance. I can hardly feel it in my fingertips.

———•◆•———

For the first time, Claire and I don't have sex when she comes over. We lie in bed and don't touch. She keeps all of her clothes on, and

I lie next to her in my boxer briefs. I think she's here to tell me that we can't do this anymore, and I don't know if I should stop her.

"Is this OK?" she asks, "that we just lie here?"

"I guess."

Doug is out on another ride, this time in some sort of nighttime hot rod parade. He'd told me the other day that he was excited about it. He was going to ride Cashmere.

"Doug thinks we should move," she says. "We've lived in the house long enough, we can sell it for a good profit and get something nicer."

"What did you say?"

"I said, 'Whatever you want.'"

We lie still. Eventually, I get cold and get under the covers. But Claire, in her clothes, doesn't need to.

"What would you have wanted me to say?"

"Whatever you want." I say. She thinks I'm just repeating her answer, but I'm not.

I roll over onto my side, slide an arm under her shirt and across her bare belly. I settle my hand there in the loose nest of her stomach. I squeeze and poke to tickle her, but she doesn't laugh. I listen for her breath, sliding in and singing out of her nostrils, but I pick up something else. Down the block, I can hear a guttural sound, almost like an animal. Its growling grows louder and louder. I imagine Doug on his Night Rod, the machine flinging itself across the pavement. Even from so far away, the noise of it fills my empty house.

BETWEEN HERE AND THERE

MORNING SHIFT:

Waysun Tsai has a fat catalog of daydreams. He flips through them
subconsciously, conjuring and developing each in turn.

He writes one now, about moving into the sewers and living
without paying rent, creating a bohemian existence beneath the
manufacturing town of Kaiping in the Guangdong province. There
he could tap into the city's utility grid and live as an underground
king. Hot girls from dark nightclubs he doesn't even know about
would visit him after closing time.

He crafts this daydream as he lifts one mug from a palette of two dozen identical mugs. He inspects it for cracks the way an enemy looks for weaknesses in an opponent. His gray shoulder-to-ankle smock is an immaculate invisibility cloak. He blends with the machinery and workers around him. He is uniform, except for the stain on the inside right wrist of his smock, which he uses to wipe away imperfections in the clay.

Another palette arrives. He lifts a single mug again, wipes at a spot in the paint and places it down. He finishes the daydream's script, in which he pays the police a handsome sum to allow him to live in peace.

As the next palette arrives he lets it pass. Another passes. Waysun eyes the subject of so many daydreams. Her name is Li Wei and every day she wears beneath her smock a shirt with a collar that folds and flies around her neckline, always in a flower print and always in such bright colors that it seems as though petals have been woven into the fabric, that she is a woman of such light and fertility that the flowers grow and glow from her skin.

Waysun has so many daydreams about Li Wei that sometimes they bleed into each other. Waysun wins the lottery and is able to buy an extended vacation with Li Wei to Australia, but her abusive alcoholic uncle is on their flight. Waysun considers fighting the uncle for saying so many rude things to Li Wei, but instead he calmly talks the uncle down and gets him to face his struggles with the bottle. Unfortunately, the plane's pilot has a heart attack and Waysun has to make flying the plane priority number one, instead of saving the pilot's life, because Li Wei and her uncle have a lifetime to catch up on and family is most important.

This crossbreeding of fantasies happens a lot when Li Wei wears her white shirt with purple flowers along the broad collar. She wears that shirt today.

CIGARETTE BREAK:

Waysun and Li Wei go for brief walks around the block for the ten-minute respite commonly known as a cigarette break. They share a bottle of juice, both because Li Wei never remembers to bring her own and because Waysun likes the smell of the lotion residue Li Wei's hands leave behind. He once daydreamed that it smelled of cut flowers, because it really smells of sweat-sweetened skin. The streets of Kaiping are filled with delivery trucks, large skronking metallic masses that are the true citizens of Kaiping. Machinery is more alive here than people.

On their walk, Li Wei talks about Thomas her boyfriend, the Chinese boy with the American name. To his friends Waysun describes Thomas as a pretty boy, which is how he describes every man he thinks more handsome than himself, which is how he thinks of nearly every man.

As they cross an angular steel bridge the wind from the river below makes them both shiver. Waysun walks with his head down as Li Wei admits that she and Thomas have been fighting. Or, more accurately, she thinks Thomas is avoiding her. Waysun offers an example of how he handled a situation with his ex-girlfriend Jiang Li (Jiang Li does not exist, is a sliver left over from a pre-Li Wei daydream). The story makes Li Wei laugh, and as they approach the plant again she throws her hands to her waist and says, "You're so weird, Waysun!" And they both laugh. Waysun looks up and sees Li Wei with her brilliant purple-flower collar propped high on her neck and her thin black hair around her ears and the glacial riverside factories of Kaiping behind her and he thinks that this is the difference between passion and passionless.

SECOND SHIFT:

By his count, Waysun has inspected 344 mugs by 11am. Counting is how he concentrates. He has done it all while refining his newest, most crystal clear daydream to date. In it, he is in a taxi coming home from a concert. He is alone and slightly drunk, feeling both free and melancholic. As the cab passes under a bridge, he looks to his left and sees Li Wei and Thomas. They are both standing solid, eight thugs yelling and pointing at them with snake-shaped knives. Waysun allows the taxi to proceed half a block down, hands the driver a pocket full of cash and tells him to keep the car running.

By the time he arrives back at the scene Thomas the pretty boy is propped up by two of the thugs, bleeding from his nose and mouth, and asking for mercy. Li Wei is weeping. Waysun runs as fast as he can—which is faster than he actually can—steps twice on the trunk of a parked car and, silently, flips and kicks one of the men holding Thomas. Jumping, spinning and striking—all silently and in complete control—he defeats three more thugs. He turns to Li Wei and commands her to pick up the whimpering Thomas, whose carefully coiffed hair is now in ruins, and run a half-block down where a cab is waiting to take them to the hospital. She knows by the look in his eye that she cannot say no. Halfway to the cab, Li Wei cries out for Waysun to come with them, but Waysun just yells, "You must go!"

When she cannot see them anymore, he defeats the rest of the gang with swift and powerful eagle claws to the throat, one for each thug. Later, he arrives at the hospital with flowers.

A palette of new mugs comes down the line. Each one reads: "A&E Investigative Reports with Bill Kurtis. The Closest You'll Get to the Truth."

LUNCH BREAK:

Waysun and Li Wei take their break together in a small garden behind the factory. The tall grass and purple reeds feel out of place among the giant steel boxes of the plant, like forgotten teenage tattoos. Li Wei sits across a table from Waysun and they both eat chicken with peppers and rice. They talk music, politics and bosses. They counsel each other on small spats with coworkers or friends. Waysun, over the course of the lunch, realizes he is happy to be Li Wei's friend. To be her friend means that he is able to be with someone so beautiful as to make Kaiping seem like paradise. In his daydreams, Li Wei is in the top three most beautiful women he would like to save from a gang of thugs. And to be friends with her, he decides, is more gift than curse. He smiles at her.

"Waysun, why are you always smiling?!" she says.

"Why not?" he replies.

She laughs. He smiles. She slaps his arm and looks down, sees the small stain on the inside of his right cuff.

She slides her hand inside his sleeve to pinch at the spot, the delicate back of her hand skims soft like wind against the sensitive inside of his wrist. "What is this from?" she asks.

Waysun says, "Uh, huh huh. Umm…heh heh huh huh uh."

"Waysun? What is wrong with you?"

"Oh," he says. "It's where I wipe the mugs. It's what I use to scrub off the imperfections."

"Huh," she says. She bows her head and pulls his sleeve to her face so that his hand enters the soft jungle of her hair. She wipes her nose with the spot.

"I hate my nose," she says. "Did it work?" And Waysun forgets all of that just-happy-to-be-friends talk.

"Nothing is that powerful," he daydreams.

AFTERNOON SHIFT:

Waysun refines his technique on the thugs in his new, slowly perfecting daydream. In each new version he's slightly skinnier, slightly faster, but also slightly more vulnerable. He can't decide if he should be stabbed or not, if it would be better for him to arrive at the hospital under his own power but in need of medical attention. He needs to make Thomas the pretty boy look entirely unheroic in relief.

Despite glances at Li Wei and the continued refinement of this story, Waysun cannot keep his concentration. With each mug he inspects, he reads the American name on the mug: Bill Kurtis. Waysun does not know what A&E Investigative Reports is, but he can read English well enough to be impressed that it has something to do with truth. He wonders if there is a way to know Li Wei's true feelings for him without asking her, without forcing a make-or-break moment, a moment that would surely break him.

He begins to feel worse about himself, about his unrequited desires, and how they are a betrayal of his friendship. In his daydreams, he becomes slower, doughier, less heroic. More real.

He lifts and stares at a gleaming mug with the name "Bill Kurtis" emblazoned along its rounded edge. He wonders, "Who is this Bill Kurtis guy? How can he be so popular that they are making thousands of mugs with his name on it?" When the buzzer sounds and it's time for Waysun to leave, he unfastens one button on his smock and slides a Bill Kurtis mug inside, unbuckles his belt and loops it through the mug handle, and refastens everything. He walks to the exit, where Li Wei waits.

CLOSING TIME:

Waysun and Li Wei walk across the same angular, steel bridge to Li Wei's bus stop. The wind now has an icy spike and carries with it the smell of diesel fuel and freshly killed fish. The two say little, but occasionally smile at each other. On the other side of the bridge Waysun can smell Li Wei's sweet sweat and fruit shampoo and thinks that must be the scent he would know by heart if they were truly in love.

"What did you think about today?" Li Wei asks. It's how they end every day, a customary question before he leaves her at her bus stop.

"I kept thinking about that Bill Kurtis guy on the mugs that came through," he says. "Just wondering what it's like to have that many people like you."

"Mmmm," says Li Wei.

"What about you, what did you think about today?" he asks. They both smile and chuckle, because her response is always the last thing either of them will say to each other, besides good-bye, until tomorrow.

"I was thinking," she laughs. "Wouldn't it be great if you didn't have to see all of this shit on the streets all day and all of these ugly buildings? I think I'd like to live on my own, underground. I really would."

"We should go to dinner sometime."

Li Wei is surprised by Waysun's response. It's out of character with both their relationship and their routine.

"Tonight?"

Waysun nods and shrugs at the same time.

"I told you, I have a boyfriend."

"I know, but I could defeat him."

This is the first time Waysun has let his daydreams slip into the mainstream of his life. He panics, and instantly begins daydreaming that this moment, unfolding now with Li Wei frowning amiably at him, is not happening, that he never said anything, and that he is walking home as he should.

"Defeat him in what?" Waysun is surprised by the sincerity of her question.

"Anything, really," he says. "But I was thinking kung fu."

Li Wei laughs.

"You're so weird, Waysun!"

And with nothing left to say to each other, Waysun turns and walks back toward the factory to catch his bus, all the while trying to craft a new daydream. But now, nothing comes to him.

SCREAM IN THE DARK

Marlon Hoffman climbs mountains in his dreams; sharp, black terrain that would be invisible were not lined with glowing phosphorescent ferns and vines that hum with energy. There are no horizons. Just upward, rocky climbs. Night after night, he lies down to sleep in his bed and ends up here, on this endless trail. The sounds all around him—a never ending whistling terror— assure him that it's just a matter of time before a ghost appears. He patiently climbs.

The first ghost Marlon ever saw was his Uncle Johnny. The two of them didn't have much to say to each other in life, Uncle Johnny a schoolteacher who had little patience for kids during his off time. They exchanged shrugs.

"Hey Uncle Johnny," Marlon said.

"Hello."

"How are you feeling?"

"Fine."

"What's new?"

"Just getting by."

Uncle Johnny looked the same as he did in life, though his skin appeared to trap light. His pores—little black holes full of little dark matter—gave him a vague countenance.

"All right, well, I'll see you soon then," Marlon said.

"Sounds about right." And Uncle Johnny walked on.

Marlon, 19 and very much alive, if not lively, had never been a gloomy kid. He read comic books and played Dungeons & Dragons, but his concern with immortality wasn't dreary. He was more interested in its logistics. What do you do with yourself when everyone you've known has died? Or conversely, if you've died, and everyone you've known is still alive.

Marlon's dream world comes in neon magenta, fluorescent green, DayGlo orange and a velvety purple. It comes in colors that are bright and clear and strike him as though he's never seen them before. But it is also black. It would be better to say it is black, but also those other colors. It is both the black of absence and the black of negation. It is a black of ocean on moonless nights. It is a black Marlon finds incomprehensible.

———•◦•———

"This is where ghosts live," Marlon taps on his temple. He's speaking with his eight-year-old niece Phoebe before Thanksgiving dinner.

"In your brain?"

"Close enough," says Marlon. "I visit them in my dreams."

"So are you a ghostbuster?"

"No," says Marlon. "I just bug them to talk with me. I'm a ghostpester."

It is exchanges like this one that will lead a teenage Phoebe to tell her boyfriends, "You have to meet my Uncle Marlon. He's totally freaky, but really cool."

"So how do you know they're really ghosts and not just

dreams?" Phoebe, as precocious as ever, has asked her uncle the question most adults never ask him. Marlon is startled by this bright little girl who wants to know so much about the dead.

"Well, the first time it happened, I talked with my uncle, and then a friend, and I knew it was real. I don't know. It was real."

Marlon won't tell her the story about the first time it happened. The story is this:

Last year, a 17-year-old kid named Leron Aucone came to Scream in the Dark Haunted House with his friends. Drunk off liquor bought by his older brother, Leron wandered through the haunted house like it was his—as though his parents owned the place and he could do whatever he liked. He found an employee-only staircase and climbed it to the third floor, where a balcony full of ghouls harangued the passersby below. He entered the balcony single-minded, wanting to amuse his friends who were about to cross the bridge below. Without thinking, he shoved one of the ghouls aside. The cheap balcony railing gave way, and the ghoul—a costumed 19-year-old Nick Collier—fell the two stories to the floor. Those in the room at the time thought it was part of the show, the frantic moan that came from deep in Nick's gut as he fell; the way he lay still on the wooden floor, dry-ice smoke swirling around him, his dark hair lit by the green spotlights. He looked like a decoration, his body just another piece of scenery built to frighten.

Marlon Hoffman and Nick Collier were new friends of little more than a year, which defined it as a particular kind of friendship; that is, one without worry. They'd worked together at the haunted house the year before, and stayed friends through the next season.

Nick didn't die right away; he was in a coma for a week with massive head trauma. The night Marlon received a call with the news, he slept for exactly one hour.

The dreams began that night. He found himself standing, lucid but confused, in this new land, like it was the first day of school.

After bumping into Uncle Johnny, Marlon heard Nick's voice. He couldn't see him, but his voice seemed to be coming from up ahead, as though Marlon only had to catch up to see him. So he began walking, because then he was at the bottom of the mountain, and the slope was easy-going. As he climbed, Nick's voice grew clearer. And the more Marlon drove his toes into the sooty terrain, the better he could hear him. Until he heard Nick say:

"Don't be sad. I'm fine."

"That's ridiculous."

"Why?"

"My Uncle Johnny just said the same thing, and he's dead."

Nick stepped out of the woods and into the clearing. His face had become a thick gray.

"Check this out," Nick said. "I got superpowers that let me talk to people in their dreams."

"I couldn't believe it when I heard about it. I want to do something for you."

"Don't be sad," Nick said. "I'm psyched."

"Where are we?"

"It's not so bad here."

"But you're not dead. Why are you here?"

When Marlon woke up the next morning, his face was soft and clammy from crying through the night. The next day, Marlon sat with Nick's family in the intensive care unit's visiting ward, an alcove of pink furniture and low lighting. He found himself thrust into a family tragedy like a guilty party. When he met Nick's parents, he apologized again and again, though everyone knew there was nothing to be done.

"Tell us about Nick," his mother said, and Marlon found himself remembering everything about him, story after story to tell, the mundane suddenly meaningful, mediocre jokes turned riotous. It discomfited Marlon to remember everything so fondly, to relate his friendship with Nick as though it were accompanied by a laugh track.

He told a story about a time the two of them had gone to a party, Nick as the designated driver. Marlon had become so drunk that he couldn't go home and face his parents, so Nick stayed up with him in an all-night Dunkin' Donuts, feeding him cruller after cruller. When Marlon finally vomited, splattering the pink and brown furniture, Nick said, "OK, you're ready to go home," and drove him to his house as the streetlamps clicked off.

"Hold on a second," Nick's dad said. He was crying.

"He took care of people," his mom said.

The story wasn't true, but Marlon thought it captured Nick's spirit. The truth was he'd seen that spirit in Nick, but didn't know him long enough to have a tale to illustrate it. The impulse to tell the truth was not as great as the fear of being left off the page.

Over the course of the next few days, Marlon brought Nick's parents bottled water and bananas from the hospital cafeteria. He sat with them and told them more stories, often untrue or embellished, and wondered what the harm was. Or he sat with them in silence, as other families, sometimes only there for a few heavy hours, sat on the other side of the room.

The day before Nick died, the doctors told his family it would happen. The numbers were getting worse, there was nothing they could do to reduce the pressure in Nick's skull. The machines couldn't lie. Nick's mother asked Marlon if he wanted to see Nick one last time before he died. Marlon, alone, approached the automatic doors. He first pressed the large square button to the side to open them, then depressed the valve to its right, filling his palms with antiseptic. He walked into the fluorescent hallway of the intensive care unit, past Nick's room on the left, unable to recognize his friend's swollen face, bandages around his head like a gauzy beehive. He found himself standing in the middle of the room, training his eyes on various beds, meeting with all kinds of injury and debilitation. Getting lost in the hospital, he thought, was a punishment he hadn't prepared for. The horror of it settled into his bones. He made his way out again.

Nick's mother asked him if he'd had enough time.

"Yeah," he lied.

It was then that Marlon decided to do what he planned on never doing. He told Nick's mother about the dream he'd had, how he'd seen Nick, and Nick had told him that he was happy, and that he was OK with everything.

"He seemed at peace," Marlon said. Nick's mother was crying.

"You don't have to tell me these things," she said, "they don't make me feel better."

"But I don't think it was just a dream. I really think he was talking to me."

"Thank you, Marlon," she said. But there was nothing in her tone to make him believe her.

———•+•+•———

Most of the ghosts Marlon has met are pleasant, happy to have company. Nick has never since visited him, and his long walks along the incandescent paths feel like clichés only dreams feel comfortable scripting. Marlon met a rancher once, walking funny without his horse. He ran into a monk with a shaved head, confused and helpless in this new mythology. But the ghosts slowly faded and have been gone for so long now, that he has almost forgotten what they look like. Marlon has scaled the obsidian mountain again and again. There's always a fluorescence in the air, like the vines and ferns and other plants are releasing tanks of gas. He hears the ghost noises but never sees them. His path a lonely one, he has no company.

"Hello!" Marlon yells in his dream. "Hey ghosts! I'm not hunting you! I'm not violent! I'm just a guy!"

The whistling palpitates, grows louder and pinches Marlon's ears. It focuses into a single pitch, a scream. Marlon wakes up.

———•+•+•———

Marlon babysits Phoebe while Hilary and her husband are at a holiday dinner party. Phoebe, uninterested in the board games Marlon has brought along, demands to know more about the ghosts. Marlon describes the mountain, the black solitude, the gleaming plant life. As he talks, Phoebe becomes excited. To her, the land of the dead is exotic. Marlon has failed to see it that way.

For him, it is an unending maze.

"So is there one ghost you're looking for?" Phoebe asks.

"I don't know. There was."

"Well, I know that if I was there I would definitely look for Peter Del Calzo."

"Who?"

"He's a kid who was in my class last year. He got leukemia and died."

"That is so fucking sad."

"Uncle Marlon! Don't curse!"

"No, it's cool, Phoebe. You're allowed to curse over this stuff."

Phoebe has an idea. She takes her uncle by the hand, leading him like a tractor into her room. She pulls down the shade, blocking out any glare from the streetlight. From her closet, she pulls out a package of neon tubing, the kind kids wear on Halloween or at park festivals. Unraveling the different colors, she begins to lay them over the dresser, across her headboard and around her nightstand. She implores her Uncle Marlon to help, and soon the two have strung the 20 feet of neon plastic around her bed, a little oasis of dull light.

"Is this what it looks like?"

"Exactly," says Marlon.

"OK, then let's lie down and wait for the ghosts to come."

Phoebe and Marlon rest on their backs, his feet hanging off the end of the bed. Phoebe's comic-book eyes, wide open and anticipatory, slowly begin to droop. Marlon watches her fall asleep, relieved. Part of him believed her excitement could summon the ghosts to her bedroom. He stares at the ceiling, wondering why, nearly a year later, he's ceased feeling sad about his friend.

———•—•———

That night, the vines and ferns are burning bright; it almost hurts Marlon's eyes to walk among them. Sensing he is getting nowhere, he diverges. He turns right, directly into the neon jungle, crossing through the thicket, the plants scratching, leaving phosphorescent bits attached to his clothes and skin. The howling, here, is softer. He emerges into a clearing, a wide ring of darkness where a crowd of ghosts has gathered. None of them speak, or seem to look at him or each other.

He calls out, "Hey, is there a kid named Peter Del Calzo here? Anyone know a kid named Peter?"

Nothing, again, but the soft howling answers him. He asks, for the first time, "Nick Collier? Nick, are you here?"

He continues to make his way through the crowd, staring into the eyes of each of the ghosts, who in turn seem to barely register him as present. It's a horror, the site of all of these dark bodies. He considers horror and bereavement as two sides of the same coin, both products of the befuddling act of living. None of these ghosts seem to get it. He moves on to the other side of the clearing, back among the neon thicket. It's quiet in the forest. After walking for what seems like hours and scratching through the vegetation, Marlon is covered in remnants of light, his clothes and skin glowing against the black absence, looking exactly like the lively ghosts he'd always imagined as a child, before Nick died and he came here. Back before he knew better.

ACKNOWLEDGMENTS

Thanks to Zach Dodson for the fantastic design. Additional thanks to the following folks: Mama and Papa Mess, Dave Mess, John Davin, Pete Coco, Patrick Somerville, Nathan Keay, Rob Funderburk, Elizabeth Crane, Todd Dills, John Huston, Joe Meno, Abraham Levitan, Fred Sasaki, Scott Snyder, The Creative Stenography Institute, Brian Evenson, Stuart Dybek, John McNally, Brian Costello, Jeremy Sosenko and Sam Axelrod. And thanks to everyone who has come out to the Dollar Store and to Tim, Jessica and Lawrence at the Hideout. And finally, if any of the stories here strike you as containing genuine moments of love, then you and I both owe a huge thanks to the most beautiful Maria Villanueva.

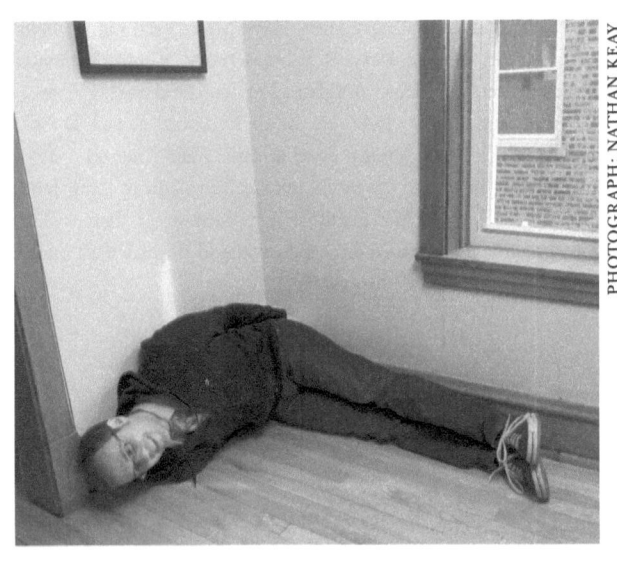

ABOUT THE AUTHOR

Jonathan Messinger is the former editor of THISisGRAND, a web magazine filled with creative non-fiction about Chicago's rapid transit. In 2004 he founded The Dollar Store Show, a monthly literary and comedy show at Chicago's legendary Hideout saloon, and the show has sold out since November 2005. He currently works as the Books editor for *Time Out Chicago* and co-publishes *featherproof* books. He's toured Canada and the U.S., performed in numerous venues including Serendipity Theatre's 2nd Story, the Red Rover Reading Series, Funny Ha Ha, the Around the Coyote Arts Festival and the Poetry Center of Chicago's No Love for Love show with Ira Glass. He also wrote a story called **The Eight Permutations of the Binoculars of Power**, which goes like this:

1 A housewife in Winnetka, Illinois gazes out her window after completing a yoga DVD workout. She notices a van with two small windows in back, parked down the street. Each day, for the next two days, she peels back the curtain like a piece of dead skin and stares at the van. On the fourth day, she digs out her husband's hunting binoculars and peers into the van's windows. She can see two men sitting back-to-back. One of them hunches over surveillance recording equipment, large headphones like Frisbees clamped on his ears. The other gazes directly at her through a pair of even larger binoculars. They wear Kevlar jackets. "Fuck it," sighs the housewife. "I'm tired of running."

2 A young girl spends an afternoon staring at the sun through a pair of binoculars, because she has read that is the path to becoming a prophet.

3 A man gives his son a pair of binoculars for his 14th birthday. The boy, unsure of what to do with them, tosses them in a shoebox with old army-man figurines and radio mix-tapes from summers past. The old toys grow uncomfortable in the company of the binoculars as a rumor spreads that the binoculars can peer into their souls.

4 Jimmy Fallon thinks his pair of binoculars is a tiny military tank.

5 A man and his younger girlfriend watch Guns N' Roses from Row P of section 309 in the upper deck grandstand of the United Center. The man watches the band through a pair of high-resolution binoculars while his girlfriend dances beside him. Their enjoyment of the show is about to end, however, because despite the younger girlfriend's pleadings, he refuses to hand over the binoculars. He does not want her to see how old Axl Rose looks.

6 A squirrel finds a pair of binoculars and carries them to the top of a tree. He becomes the most powerful squirrel in the world.

7 A brother and sister are quarantined in their respective bedrooms to protect them from a vicious plague. The last time they saw someone alive, it was Mrs. Aucone across the street. Blood gurgled from her throat and her skin appeared the color of worn dollar bills. The brother and sister talk to each other through their bedroom walls. They play games like 20 questions, trivial pursuit with no board, and invented games like, What Face Am I Making Right Now? The brother confesses all his sins to his sister, who refuses to listen.

8 A man and a woman together decide it is necessary to spice up their sex lives. The woman suggests bringing toys into the bedroom, to which the man does not so much agree as not say anything, which the woman construes as agreement. Two nights later, when they know they will both be at home for the evening, they are to each bring one item into the bedroom.

8 The woman brings with her into the bedroom a beaded dildo still in a package that reads: "The Scintillator: You're in for a bumpy ride." The man panics when he sees this, for obvious reasons. The woman opens The Scintillator's packaging and holds it like a glass of fine wine. She sniffs it, tips it toward the man, and tosses it lightly on the bed. She asks what he has brought. The man announces he has brought with him a pair of binoculars. The woman asks what in hell they're supposed to do with a pair of binoculars in their own bedroom. The man, clearly improvising, says he doesn't know what they're going to do with them… but he can't wait to find out. For him, he lies, imagination is sexy.

7 The sister does not listen to her brother, who lies and lies because he needs a listener. She sits at her windowsill, a pair of old toy binoculars in her hands and pressed to her window. Three days ago she discovered a boy a year older than her with wild hair and the noticeable beginnings of a beard quarantined in a room down the street. The brother begs her forgiveness and she grants it over and over again, finding it easy to dole out because she is not there. She is, in her mind, in the apartment down the street with her boy with wild hair who is looking a little green, a bit like his skin is made of old dollar bills.

6 The most powerful squirrel in the world suffers from vertigo because he doesn't know how to use the binoculars; and he also develops a narcissistic obsession with his own magnified image in the binocular lens. He hasn't eaten for days. Other squirrels grow questioning of his power.

5 The man relents and hands over his high-resolution binoculars to his younger girlfriend and he can instantly feel himself wither in her eyes. But he's wrong. His younger girlfriend is untroubled by how agéd Axl Rose looks. What kills them, is that Buckethead has still got it.

4 Jimmy Fallon thinks his pair of binoculars could actually be a large military tank for an army of tiny people. He grows very frightened.

3 An army-man figurine in a shoebox under a 14-year-old boy's bed, waits until nighttime. He creeps behind a pile of mixtapes and opens fire on a lens, because he's done too many things that he's not proud of in the name of his country to be judged by some Johnny-Come-Lately Soulseer.

2 An old man cherishes his pair of binoculars, spends his evenings on a porch looking at the constellations, his old fingers too inexact now to calibrate a telescope. He's heard that staring at the stars is a path to longevity.

1 A husband in Winnetka, Illinois, comes home from a business trip to find a DVD workout tape playing to an empty room. Upstairs, he finds his wife hanging from a door frame, a binocular rope wrapped around her neck as a noose. He stills her swaying body. "You'll pay for this," he says, and opens fire on a van parked across the street.

THIS IS A CATALOG

featherproof books is an indie press based in Chicago, publishing strange and beautiful fiction and nonfiction and post-, trans-, and inter-genre tragicomedy. Available at bookstores everywhere and featherproof.com.

History In One Act:
A novel of 9/11
by William M. Arkin

Tiny
by Mairead Case

Sunshine On an
Open Tomb
by Tim Kinsella

Weeping Gang Bliss
Void Yab-Yum
by Devendra Banhart

On the Back of Our
Images, vol. I
by Luc Dardenne

The Spud
by Brielle Brilliant

Mammother
by Zachary Schomburg

From the Inside
by John Henry Timmis IV

I'm Fine, But You
Appear to Be Sinking
by Leyna Krow

The Inborn Absolute
by Robert Ryan

MAKE X
by various artists

**The Tennessee Highway
Death Chant**
by Keegan Jennings Goodman

All Over and Over
by Tim Kinsella

Erratic Fire, Erratic Passion
by Pasha Malla & *Jeff Parker*

See You in the Morning
by Mairead Case

The Minus Times
COLLECTED

**The Minus Times
Collected**
by various artists

**The Karaoke Singer's
Guide to Self-Defense**
by Tim Kinsella

**The Universe in
Miniature in Miniature**
by Patrick Somerville

Daddy's
by Lindsay Hunter

The Awful Possibilities
by Christian TeBordo

Scorch Atlas
by Blake Butler

AM/PM
by Amelia Gray

boring boring boring boring
boring boring boring
by Zach Plague

This Will Go Down on
Your Permanent Record
by Susannah Felts

Sons of the Rapture
by Todd Dills

The Enchanters vs.
Sprawlburg Springs
by Brian Costello

HIDING OUT

decoys by jonathan messinger

After another bomb dropped and a mountain crumbled and the horizon cracked, I turned to my wife and said, "I think we can get you and me out of here but I'm not so sure about the kids." And she said, "We don't have kids, remember?"

I knew then that something was wrong, that the impacts had jarred something loose, physical or psychological, I didn't know. Regardless, I wish I'd said something else, because the topic of kids—whether we should have them, whether we should adopt them, whether another man should come in and sire them if I wasn't willing to do it myself—has been a wound in our marriage for all two years of it. And that's the last thing our marriage needed at that moment, after another bomb dropped, killing off the electricity and sending schrapnel through the two windows of our apartment and half a tree through the west wall.

"You always do this," she said. "You always make a point of showing how easy our lives are because we don't have kids."

I tried to explain to her that I didn't mean anything by it, but as she sloughed a pile of water bottles into a duffel bag I caught sight of the Gleesons across the street. They ran screaming from their house, the father with a rifle, the mother and son with long sharp knives.

"I can't remember," I said. "Do we like the Gleesons?"

"We don't know anyone named Gleeson," she said. I didn't know what was happening to me.

"Well, then who lives across the street from us?"

"You mean the McCabes? Jesus, you babysit their son Michael."

I didn't respond to this bit of information, enrapt in the whole scene in front of me. There were cars overturned and stumbling victims holding various damaged body parts. It was clearly the end of something and the beginning of something else, but I wasn't sure what.

The lovely family across the street had turned into marauding savages. Mr. McCabe was threatening a young man with his rifle and Michael, surprisingly skilled with a knife, was slicing a dead creature—a rat, a cat, a fatted and half-hibernated squirrel, maybe—into clean cuts of steak. I stayed mum, not sure if I was hallucinating the whole thing.

"Put this on, it'll help you breathe," my wife said.

She gave me a sort of surgical mask, and when I looked at her she was already wearing one, along with goggles and a nylon biohazard suit.

"Where did you get all of this stuff?" I asked. I was still in shorts and a T-shirt, while my wife had turned into a hazmat technician. She didn't answer. We made our way to the stairs and as we descended, smoke burned at my eyes. We tripped over things both soft and sharp. It was like I'd never been down this staircase before, even though it was the most important staircase of my life.

As my wife took my hand and led me out onto the sidewalk, I asked a question.

"Is this an attack or an apocalypse?"

"It's the same thing at this point," she said, as she ducked behind a tree and a kitchen knife, thrown by Mrs. McCabe, whizzed by with a dry sound, clanking against the fence.

I realized at this point that I'd gone through all of this not knowing what to think of it. There was my wife, and our neighbor had just tried to kill her, which I thought was wrong. And there was our apartment that we'd have to abandon, which left me a little sad. But then I remembered that it was my wife's place first and I had moved in, and that had created an awkward dynamic, so I was fine with letting it crumble.

I gazed down the street and, as leaves fell in a silent storm and funnel clouds touched down on the horizon, I felt a pinch of regret. I knew I'd be with my wife for the rest of the time we could survive, but the rest of our days would be spent protecting ourselves from random attacks, scavenging for food, touching through the prophylactic membranes of biohazard suits, our kisses just warm exchanges of breath through filtered masks. I wouldn't be able to refer to this as our salad days.

And there was Mr. McCabe. Right in front of me—how had this happened? He pointed his shotgun at my chest, yelled about giving him everything we had. I thought that he was probably a good man. I could smell the gun metal in front of my face and it made my teeth ache. I looked at his face and it seemed like some of his skin had melted. Could that be right?

My wife rose and stood by his side, as if in friendship. At first I thought it was betrayal, but then she lifted a hand and brought a rock down on the back of Mr. McCabe's skull. Just like that. He fell quickly. Mrs. McCabe began screaming, mourning the loss of her husband and her knife, both lying next to our fence.

"We have to keep moving," my wife said. Her voice sounded strange through the mask. It made me sad that my wife's voice came across clear, stale and robotic. Mrs. McCabe, across the way, was wailing for her husband, sounding human. I could hear how much she loved him.

"I think we can get you and me out of here but I'm not so sure about the kids," I said.

My wife, she grabbed me by the hand, and we ran right down the street. I decided that if I was going to have an opinion about all this, it was that I would be glad to be with my wife. And it wouldn't be an "at the very least we have each other," or a "this is all we have," sentiment, it would be an "I am a happy man because I am holding my wife's hand," feeling. Despite it all. So we ran away from the funnel clouds, away from the apartment that was never mine, away from all of that past destruction, and toward some new disaster entirely.

www.ingramcontent.com/pod-product-compliance
Lightning Source LLC
Chambersburg PA
CBHW020120180626
46812CB00006B/2668